"I Don't Care What Anyone Says, I Don't Want You Protecting Me,"

said Clea.

"You sure about that?" Ryan asked.

"Positive," she tossed back. It was bad enough the man made her hormones act up. The last thing she needed was to have him trailing her back to her apartment, sticking himself into her life.

He reached out and tucked a strand of hair behind her ear. "That's too bad. Your not wanting me, I mean. It would have made us being roommates a lot more interesting."

"Roommates?" she repeated. "What are you talking about? We're not going to be roommates."

"Sure we are. Because from now on, Duchess, wherever you go, I go. That's what a bodyguard does."

Dear Reader,

MEN! This month Silhouette Desire goes man-crazy with six of the sexiest, heart-stopping hunks ever to come alive on the pages of a romance novel.

Meet May's MAN OF THE MONTH, love-wary secret agent Daniel Lawless, in *The Passionate G-Man,* the first book in Dixie Browning's fabulous new miniseries, THE LAWLESS HEIRS. Metsy Hingle's gallant hero protects an independent lady in danger in the last book of the RIGHT BRIDE, WRONG GROOM series, *The Bodyguard and the Bridesmaid.* Little bitty Joeville, Montana, has more tall, dark and rugged ranchers than any other town west of the Mississippi. And Josh Malone has more sex appeal than all of 'em put together in *Last of the Joeville Lovers,* the third book in Anne Eames's MONTANA MALONES series.

In *The Notorious Groom,* Caroline Cross pairs the baddest boy ever to roam the streets of Kisscount with the town virgin in a steamy marriage of convenience. The hero of Barbara McCauley's *Seduction of the Reluctant Bride* is one purebred Texas cowboy fixin' to do some wife-wranglin'—this new groom isn't about to miss a sultry second of his very own wedding night. Yeehaw! Next, when a suddenly wealthy beauty meets the owner of the ranch next door, he's wearing nothing but a Stetson and a smile in Carol Grace's *The Heiress Inherits a Cowboy.*

Silhouette Desire brings you the kind of irresistible men who make your knees buckle, your stomach flutter, your heart melt…and your fingers turn the page. So enjoy our lineup of spectacular May men!

Regards,

Melissa Senate

Senior Editor
Silhouette Books

Please address questions and book requests to:
Silhouette Reader Service
U.S.: 3010 Walden Ave., P.O. Box 1325, Buffalo, NY 14269
Canadian: P.O. Box 609, Fort Erie, Ont. L2A 5X3

METSY HINGLE
THE BODYGUARD AND THE BRIDESMAID

SILHOUETTE *Desire*®

™ Published by Silhouette Books

America's Publisher of Contemporary Romance

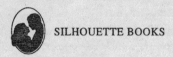

SILHOUETTE BOOKS

ISBN 0-373-76146-5

THE BODYGUARD AND THE BRIDESMAID

Books by Metsy Hingle

Silhouette Desire

Seduced #900
Surrender #978
Backfire #1026
Lovechild #1055
*The Kidnapped Bride #1103
*Switched at the Altar #1133
*The Bodyguard and the Bridesmaid #1146

*Right Bride, Wrong Groom

METSY HINGLE

is a native of New Orleans who loves the city in which she grew up. She credits the charm of her birthplace, and her own French heritage, with instilling in her the desire to write. Married and the mother of four children, she believes in romance and happy endings. Becoming a Silhouette author is a long-cherished dream come true for Metsy and one happy ending that she continues to celebrate with each new story she writes. She loves hearing from readers. Write to Metsy at P.O. Box 3224, Covington, LA 70433.

To Sandra and Michael Brown.
Two very special people, two very special friends.

Prologue

She hated weddings, Clea Mason decided, scowling at the bridal bouquet of white roses and lilies that had managed to land in her hands. Silently she cursed Ryan Fitzpatrick. If he hadn't distracted her, she never would have caught the blasted bouquet.

"Oh, Clea, you're going to be the next bride!"

"Not if I can help it," Clea muttered to her newly-married assistant, Gayle. There was no way she intended to get married—ever.

"You'll change your mind when you meet the right man. Just like I did when I met my Larry," the other woman replied dreamily before being ushered off for the garter toss.

Relieved to relinquish the spotlight, Clea glanced at her watch and frowned. *Just how long does the maid of honor need to remain at these things?* Recalling her two sisters' weddings, she nearly groaned. If memory served her correctly, she'd have to stay at least until the newlyweds left, and they didn't look like they would be going anytime soon.

Resigned to being stuck a while longer, Clea studied the guests who had turned out for the wedding of her assistant at Destinations. Most were employees of the travel agency, Clea noted. Not surprising, since the bride and groom had no family in Chicago and the agency's owners had insisted on hosting the reception. Clea paused as her gaze fixed on Ryan Fitzpatrick.

Even huddled with the tuxedo-clad groomsmen, he stood out, and not simply because of his height. The man was flat-out gorgeous, Clea admitted. With his sharp-edged features, deep blue eyes and wicked grin, he reminded her of a fallen angel. His dark hair brushed the collar of his shirt in a way that made a woman itch to run her fingers through the wayward curls, she thought, and tightened her fingers around the stem of the bouquet. As though sensing her scrutiny, Ryan looked up and flashed her that lady-killer smile.

Her traitorous pulse jumped. *Blast the man,* she thought. Turning away quickly, she barreled right into Sean Fitzpatrick. "I'm sorry," she said, taking a step back to steady herself.

"I'm not. You can run into my arms anytime," Sean informed her with a grin. He shifted his gaze to the flowers in her hands. "I was going to ask you to dance. But what do you say we just skip the dancing part and get married instead?"

"Ignore him," Michael Fitzpatrick said, shouldering his younger brother aside before she could even catch her breath. "Marry me. I'm a much better catch."

Clea laughed at their outrageous proposals, the tension inside her evaporating. Amused, she relaxed as the brothers bickered over which of them she should marry. Nephews of the owners of Destinations, the pair were familiar faces at the agency she managed and the source of more than a few fantasies among her female staff. Given their good looks and reputations with the fairer sex, Clea was grateful she'd never been tempted to engage in anything more than friendship with either man. Too bad she couldn't say the same thing about their brother Ryan. Ryan disturbed her in a way no other man had for a very long time.

"Clea, tell my thick-headed brother here that he's wasting his time," Sean insisted.

"You're *both* wasting your time," came Ryan's deep voice from behind her. "Clea isn't going to marry either one of you clowns. She's going to marry me."

Stunned, Clea whirled around. Her pulse hammered furiously as she stared at him. Mischief sparkled in his eyes as he twirled the bride's garter on his index finger. A smile played across his lips. "Marry you?" she repeated, her temper spiking at his arrogance. "Why I—"

"Can hardly wait. I know, darling. I feel the same way." And before she could utter a word of protest, he hauled her into his arms and kissed her.

One

"**I** want Clea Mason's case," Ryan said firmly. Folding his arms over his chest, he stared across the desk at his brother Michael and prepared to do battle.

Michael disengaged the speakerphone, severing the telephone connection with their aunt. He leaned back in his chair. "There is no 'case,' little brother."

Ryan bit back the temper that had been building inside him from the moment his Aunt Maggie had come on the line and told them some nut had been pestering Clea. "I may be the new kid on the block here as far as being a private investigator goes, but as a former cop I can tell you that some pervert sending Clea twisted love letters and calling her on the phone makes for a good case of harassment."

"Which is what I tried to tell Aunt Maggie," his brother replied, looking more like a lawyer than a detective in his neat white shirt and tie. "We're security specialists, Ry, not bodyguards."

"The office manager at Destinations being harassed by some guy doesn't warrant some specialized security?"

"You and I both know this isn't a security matter. It's a police matter—which is why I didn't want to take this job to begin with."

"But you did take it," Ryan pointed out.

Michael scowled at him. "When's the last time you came up against Aunt Maggie and won?" Not waiting for an answer, he continued, "Besides, what chance did I have when you sat there agreeing with everything she said?"

"I happened to think she was right. Clea needs protection." At his brother's snort, Ryan said, "Come on, Mike. You heard Aunt Maggie. This has been going on for a couple of months, and the cops haven't gotten anywhere. That's why she wanted to hire us, and it's the reason you let her bamboozle you into accepting the job. And since you did accept the job, someone needs to keep an eye on Clea. I'm volunteering."

"Seems to me you've been keeping your eye on Clea for quite some time." Michael pitched down his pen and eyed Ryan closely. "Hell, I wouldn't be at all surprised if *she* was the reason you decided to leave the LAPD and move back here to join Sean and me at the agency."

It was pretty close to the truth, Ryan admitted silently. Clea *had* played a role in his decision to come home. But as the youngest of four boys, he'd learned a long time ago not to give his brothers that kind of ammo. They'd rag him to no end if he did. "My reasons for coming home aren't the point here. Clea's safety is. I'm offering to do the job and make sure nothing happens to her."

"The 'job' would be a lot easier if we could tell Clea we were going to keep her under surveillance."

"I agree. But since she balked at the idea when Aunt Maggie suggested it, we can't. I'll just have to protect her without her knowing it." And while he was keeping her safe, who knew what would happen? A smile tickled his lips as he remembered meeting her for the first time six months ago. He had stopped in at the travel agency to visit his aunt and uncle. While he had waited, he'd been admiring the rear view of the feminine curves and legs of the woman whose back was to him.

Then she'd turned around. And wham! It hit him—that quick-fire flash of awareness. One look into those cat-green eyes, and he'd been a goner. Sure, there was lust. A man couldn't look at Clea and not want her. But it was more. There was something endearing about the swift way she moved around the office, the way she dealt with the young mother trying to stretch her travel dollars for a visit home. It touched something inside him.

He hadn't expected it, and certainly hadn't thought it would happen with her. He'd heard all about the efficient Clea. Ambitious corporate women held no appeal for him. He liked his women soft, fragile—the Suzy-Homemaker types who would be happy being a wife and producing a team of little leaguers. No way had he imagined falling for a career woman. And he certainly hadn't imagined that the woman he did fall for would take so much convincing that he was the right man for her.

"—besides, you've only been with the agency a few weeks. Hardly enough time to get your feet wet in this business."

Ryan jerked his attention back to Michael and realized he had missed half of what his brother had said to him. "Sorry. What was that you were saying?"

"I said tailing someone who knows you can be a tricky business. Both Sean and I have had more experience at it. It might be better if one of us handled this."

"No way."

"Ryan—"

He shot to his feet. Flattening his palms on the desk, he leaned in, bringing his face within inches of his brother's. "I'd say twelve years on the police force with eight of those years working under cover in vice and homicide gives me a lot of experience. So don't pull that garbage about you and Sean being older and more experienced. I'm telling you I want this case.''

''What case?'' Sean asked, breezing into the room and looking as though he had just tumbled out of bed. Some female's bed no doubt, Ryan decided, given the sleep-hungry, but sated expression on his brother's face. Making himself at home on the edge of Michael's desk, Sean drank deep and long from the steaming cup he held in his hands.

''Clea Mason's case,'' Michael replied.

Sean glanced up from his cup, his eyes sharp with interest. ''Clea The Dish is a client?''

''Not exactly,'' Michael informed him as he shoved back from his desk. He went over to the coffee setup and poured himself a cup from the pot. ''It seems some guy's been sending her twisted love letters. Last night he phoned her. Aunt Maggie was with Clea when she got the call, and from what she heard, the fellow's verbal skills leave something to be desired.''

Sean swore and crushed his empty cup. ''I'd like to get my hands on the creep.''

''You'll have to wait in line,'' Ryan informed him.

''No one's going to get a shot at the guy unless the cops catch him,'' Michael replied. Until they do, Aunt Maggie wants someone from Fitzpatrick Security to keep an eye on Clea.''

''And that someone is going to be me,'' Ryan insisted.

''Hey, wait a minute! Why do you get to have all the fun?'' Sean countered. ''Besides, I think Clea has a thing for me. Did you see the way she looked at me at that wedding reception last week? The woman's nuts about me. I certainly wouldn't object to keeping her company. I'm your man, Mike. Don't worry, I'll take good care of her.''

''The hell you will,'' Ryan said through gritted teeth. ''If anyone's going to take care of Clea, it's going to be *me*.''

Sean practically beamed at the outburst. "Face it, little brother. The lady's not interested." Pitching his empty cup into the trash can, Sean scored a ringer and pulled his fisted arm down in a victory sign before turning back to Ryan. He grinned. "Now what was it she said in answer to your proposal? Oh, yeah, I remember. Something like, 'not if you were the last man on earth.' Guess you're just not her type."

"And you think you are?" Ryan shot back.

"As a matter of fact, I do. And you know, now that I think about it, she never did turn down *my* proposal." Amusement gleamed in his eyes. "I guess that means she and I are engaged. In that case, I definitely should be the one assigned to keep her safe."

At thirty-two, he would have sworn he'd outgrown the habit of rising to his siblings' baiting, Ryan told himself. Obviously, he hadn't, because he was itching to pound his fists against his brother's grinning face. "Like hell you will," he repeated with a snarl, clenching his fists at his side.

"You know, Sean does have a point," Michael said, failing miserably to hide the smile tickling his lips. "From the look on Clea's face when you kissed her at that wedding, I'd say you're not exactly her favorite Fitzpatrick."

"Don't bet on it," Ryan told him. Clea's response to his kiss may have been brief, but there had been no mistaking that flash fire between them before she'd caught herself.

"Guess you got shortchanged on the Fitzpatrick charm, little brother," Sean needled. "Now, me on the other hand—"

"Didn't get any," Ryan fired back, then turned to Michael. "I want this case, Mike. We agreed I'd be an equal partner when I joined the agency. Well, I've been with the firm nearly a month and all I've done is shuffle papers."

"Shuffling papers is part of the job."

"But it's not all of it," Ryan argued.

Michael sighed. "Give yourself a break, Ry. From what I heard, you were handling some pretty heavy stuff before you turned in your badge."

"Handled is the right word. It's done, and now I'm ready to move on. I want to go to work."

"Kids," Michael said as though his extra three years made him ancient. "I'd think you would appreciate having some time to get used to not being a cop before having cases dumped on you."

"I don't need any time. I'm finished being a cop." He had done the best he could at the job, but the system had gotten to him. He would no sooner bring in a bust, than the criminals were back on the street. But it hadn't just been the job. He had felt something was missing in his life and realized it was family. So, he had turned in his shield, packed his bags and come home. "What I need is to work—and I don't mean more desk-jockey duty. Besides you and Sean are already tied up on other cases. It only makes sense that I get Clea."

"Hold on a second," Sean countered. "You take the check fraud case I'm working on, and I'll guard Clea's body."

Michael shook his head. "Sorry, bro. No can do. Sylvia Miller specifically requested you head that investigation."

"Ah, yes, the lovely Sylvia," Sean said, his eyes brightening at the mention of the shapely bank president. "So much for me not having any charm."

Ryan snorted. "Then it's settled. I get Clea." Standing, he decided to get going before anyone objected.

"Ry, hold on a second," Michael said.

Ryan paused, then frowned at his brother's serious expression. "Yeah?"

"Chances are this nut who's harassing Clea is harmless. That type usually is. But if he's not—if he decides he wants more of a thrill than he can get from a letter or phone call— she could be in real danger. She can't afford to have someone who isn't completely focused on the job protecting her.''

Ryan stiffened. ''You think I can't handle the job?''

''I'm saying I know you've got a thing for Clea.'' Michael held up his hand when Ryan started to protest. ''We both know becoming involved with a client screws up your judgment. You lose focus because you're no longer thinking with just your head. If that happens on this case, it's Clea who's going to pay the price. I don't want to see her get hurt.''

I'm not going to let anything happen to her and I'm not going to screw up.''

''Maybe not intentionally, but—''

''Hey, come on, Mike,'' Sean cut in as he retrieved a candy bar from his pocket and began unwrapping it. ''Clea's got better taste. Why would she fall for this guy when she can have me?''

Ryan swiped the candy from Sean's fingers, grateful for something to wrap his fist around. ''I wouldn't be so sure of that if I were you, big brother.''

''She turned down your proposal, remember?'' Sean teased.

''Haven't you heard, women often change their minds. She'll change hers.''

''Right,'' Sean quipped, giving him a disgusted look and reclaiming his half-eaten chocolate bar. ''I got a hundred bucks that says the lady turns you down flat—again.''

''You're on,'' Ryan told him. ''Let's see your green.''

Sean reached into his wallet and pulled out two fifties. He slapped them on the desk. ''What about you, Mike? You want a piece of this?''

''As a matter of fact, I do.'' He threw a crisp hundred-dollar bill onto the desk. ''I'm with Sean. I say Clea tosses you out on your can.''

Ryan dropped his own C-note onto the stack. ''Six

months from now when I slip a wedding ring on Clea's finger, I'll be back to collect that.''

A chill chased its way down Clea's spine. She spun around, unable to shake the feeling that she was being watched. Clenching and unclenching the strap of her evening bag, she glanced at the faces of the people around her. Normal faces. Just people in a crowd. And not one of them seemed to be the least bit interested in her.

It's just nerves, Clea told herself. No doubt brought on by working too many hours and not getting enough sleep. In fact, she should be at home now, making it an early night—not standing on a Chicago street corner in a crush of people waiting for the theater doors to open. She should never have agreed to accompany the Donatellis on this dinner-and-theater outing. Especially not after receiving that last phone call.

Clea shuddered, recalling that eerie whispered voice at the other end of the phone line a short while ago.

"You looked so beautiful today. I liked that red dress you were wearing. I wish I could see you right now. I need to see you. I want to be with you tonight. I want to—"

Stop it, Clea ordered herself, fighting against the panic bubbling inside her as she remembered the letters, the sound of that menacing voice telling her all the despicable things he wanted to do to her. No one was watching her. She was just edgy, she told herself, drawing in a calming breath and releasing it. Nerves. That's all it was. She had been running on overload for too long. Who wouldn't be a little tense under the same circumstances?

Of course, spying Ryan Fitzpatrick in the restaurant tonight hadn't helped. She frowned as she considered the unlikely meeting. The third time in as many weeks that the man had turned up in the same place where she was. Ever since that day at the wedding....

The wedding. Clea squeezed her eyes shut, mortified

every time she thought of his behavior at the reception and, even worse, her own shameful response to him. For a brief moment when he kissed her, sanity had deserted her. She had been unable to resist the warmth of his arms around her, the feel of his mouth moving seductively, expertly over hers. Color climbed her cheeks as she recalled how she had melted into the kiss.

It didn't matter that her loss of control had been only momentary or that no one else seemed to have noticed. Ryan had noticed. She'd seen it in the deep blue of his eyes when she'd jerked free of his embrace. And it had still been there in the satisfied curve of his lips when she'd stomped off.

How could she have been so foolish? She knew Ryan Fitzpatrick's type—the easy charmers who turned a girl's head with sweet talk and empty promises. She knew the type, and she had no desire to become involved with him or anyone like him. She had learned the hard way just how expensive and painful a relationship with a man like him could be. She still bore the scars to prove it. And she didn't care if he *did* kiss like a champ and made her heart stutter with just a look. She had no intention of becoming involved with him.

Suddenly she stiffened, feeling that uneasy prickle at the base of her neck again. She hugged her arms about herself and slowly turned around. She scanned the faces in the crowd again, not even sure who or what she expected to find. Her gaze skipped over face after face—some young, some old. Just people. Strangers waiting, as she was, to see the play. No one face, no one person stood out as anything but normal.

Frustrated, Clea shifted her gaze across the street. She narrowed her eyes at the sight of a dark-haired man leaning against a building. He seemed familiar, she thought. Then he turned his head and looked right at her. For a split second, their eyes met.

Ryan? Someone walked in front of him, blocking her view. And when the man had passed, he was gone. *So what if it is Ryan? The man's a security detective for pity's sake. He's probably working on a case.*

"Oh, look. I think they're about to open the doors," the woman next to her said.

Dismissing Ryan from her thoughts, Clea cut a glance to the glass doors of the theater entrance where a uniformed employee stood fitting a key into the lock.

"About time," someone grumbled.

The crowd stirred as the doors opened. Clea braced herself against the gentle nudge of bodies and murmured apologies as they made their way slowly toward the theater doorway. Wishing again that she had declined the Donatellis' invitation, she realized that she hadn't even seen Maggie or James since they had all left the restaurant. They must be at the front of the line waiting for her and their other guests, she decided. An errant strand escaped her upswept hairstyle, and Clea tucked it into place as she inched forward with the others.

A warm breath tickled the back of her neck, sending a chill down Clea's spine. Heart pounding, she started to turn around when the crowd shot forward again.

"I've been wanting to touch you all evening."

Fear tightened her throat, paralyzing her for long seconds, at the sound of that voice. She tried to whip around, but found herself trapped, unable to move amid the crush of bodies pushing her toward the theater entrance. Panic raced through her. "Please. I need to get through," Clea choked out the words and shoved at the man in front of her, struggling to break free.

"You'll have to wait your turn like the rest of us, sister," somebody snapped.

"You don't understand, I have to—"

"You can't escape. I'll never let you go."

The blood in her veins turned to ice as he began telling her what he wanted in that throaty whisper. She started to shove again, but a hand reached from behind her and fingers closed tightly around her breast.

Clea screamed, a bloodcurdling cry of outrage and fear that echoed in her ears. She whipped around, her elbows striking against chests, shoulders and arms. Heedless of the grunts and protests her frantic movements incited, she stared into a sea of strange faces. "Who are you?" she demanded, hating the note of hysteria climbing in her voice. "Why are you doing this to me?"

"Who are you yelling at?" an elderly gentleman asked.

She registered the cap of snow-white hair gleaming in the evening light. "Someone…someone just said something to me." She couldn't bring herself to admit that the monster had also touched her.

"Harry, did you say something to the young lady?" the woman beside him asked.

"Not me." He eyed her as though he thought she were ill.

"Then it must have been someone else," Clea insisted as people began to step around them. "You must have seen him. A man. He was standing right behind me."

The couple looked at one another and shook their heads. "Sorry. Didn't notice anyone in particular. Hard to with this kind of crowd." Draping his arm protectively around the shoulder of the woman beside him, he said, "Come on, Josie. We want to see the play."

"But wait—"

"Clea." Ryan shouldered his way to her side. "What is it? What happened?"

Relief flooded through her at the sight of him. "There was a man. He—"

"It's all right," he said, pulling her into his arms. He stroked her back, made soothing sounds, then slowly steered her away from the dwindling crowd.

"Clea! Ryan!"

Margaret Donatelli rushed over to them. "What's going on?"

Clea stepped out of Ryan's arms and went to her friend. "He was here, Maggie. At the theater."

"Who?" Margaret asked.

"The...the man who's been sending me the letters and calling me."

"What happened?" James Donatelli asked as he rushed over to join them. "I was buying theater programs, and then the next thing I knew I couldn't find Maggie or you."

"Poor Clea's had a terrible fright. Apparently the man who's been sending her those letters followed her here tonight."

"Where is he?"

"He ran away when I screamed," Clea explained.

"My God!" James exclaimed.

"Did you get a look at his face?" Ryan asked, his gaze fastening on hers. The look in his eyes was dark, determined, and not even remotely flirtatious. His cop face, she decided, remembering that he had been one. Given his fierce expression, she almost pitied the criminals who had crossed his path. The serious, focused Ryan Fitzpatrick was even more unsettling than Ryan Fitzpatrick the charmer.

"Did you get a look at his face?" Ryan repeated.

"No. He was behind me, and the crowd was too thick. I couldn't turn around. All I could do was listen."

"Did you recognize his voice?" he asked, his voice sharp, his eyes sharper, reminding her of a wolf on a hunt.

"No. He...whispered."

"What did he say?"

She rubbed her hands up and down her arms, trying to

shake off the chill inside her as she remembered what he had told her. "Things…things that he wanted to do." Clea trembled. No way could she repeat to Ryan the things the man had said when he'd touched her.

"Enough with the questions," James snapped. "Can't you see she's upset?"

"It's all right. I'm sure Ryan's only trying to help." Regaining a grip on herself, Clea straightened her shoulders. "If you two don't mind, I think I'm going to skip the theater. I just want to go home."

"You need to call the police," Ryan told her.

"I intend to. After I get home."

"You should call now so they can take your statement while everything's still fresh. Here, you can use my cell phone."

Clea ignored the phone in his outstretched hand. "I said I'll call when I get home."

"I'll give you a ride home. You can call from my car." He cupped his hand under her elbow.

Clea dug in her heels, feeling as though she were being railroaded. "What about your case?"

"My case?"

"The one you're working on. That is why you were across the street earlier, isn't it? Because you're working on some type of investigation?"

Ryan paused. His eyes darted from her to his aunt and back again. "I'm finished for tonight. So, I can take you home. While I'm there, I'll check out your apartment for you. Make sure your locks and alarm system are up to snuff."

Clea swallowed. She hadn't even considered that he could be waiting in her home for her. It had never once crossed her mind. But then, she hadn't expected him to be here at the theater tonight either.

"Heavens! You're shaking like a leaf," Maggie told her.

"You're in no condition to be by yourself tonight. You're coming home with James and me."

"Uh, Aunt Maggie. I'll see that she gets home safely. And she really should file that report with the police."

"The police will just have to wait. They haven't done anything so far." She turned to her husband. "Can you finish up things here with the marketing people from Taylor's without me?"

"I'll make our excuses. You take the car, and I'll take a taxi home." He kissed his wife. "I'll be there as soon as I can. Ryan, would you mind walking them to the car?"

"Glad to."

Maggie led her to the parking lot at a brisk pace, but she was conscious of Ryan behind them, speaking to someone on his cellular phone.

"Now when we get home, I'm going to draw you a nice hot bath, and then I want you to—"

"Aunt Maggie," Ryan cut in, his voice deep and tight. As they reached the car, he took the key from his aunt's fingers and unlocked the door. "I called the police. They're sending a unit out to speak to Clea."

"Then you'll have to call them back and tell them to come to my house, because that's where she'll be." Maggie ushered Clea into the back seat and climbed in beside her.

Ryan ducked his head inside the car. "You intend to drive from back here?"

She patted Ryan's cheek as though he were a child. "No, my dear boy, I intend for you to drive us home, and then I want you to come back here to pick up your uncle."

"I'm a security specialist, not a chauffeur," Ryan argued, but he slid into the driver's seat anyway and started the engine.

"You're also my nephew, Ryan Fitzpatrick. And you might want to remember that at least for the time being, you and your agency are on *my* payroll."

Stunned, Clea asked, "Fitzpatrick Security is working for you?"

Maggie made a face. "Yes, but given Ryan's performance here tonight, I'm beginning to wonder if I'm getting my money's worth."

Two

"**I** don't need a private investigator or a security specialist, or whatever it is he calls himself," Clea told his aunt several hours later.

"Either one works for me. Take your pick," Ryan offered from across the Donatellis' living room. He earned himself another glare. Clea had gone all stiff and prim the moment she had discovered *she* was the case he had been working on. And she had been spitting mad ever since.

"You shouldn't have hired him without consulting me."

"Someone had to do something," Maggie countered.

"I was..." She hissed out a breath. "I *am* doing something. I'm letting the police handle it. You heard the officer. They're working up a profile on the type of...on the type of person who does this sort of thing."

This sort of thing. She made it sound so civilized, Ryan thought, observing the exchange between Clea and his aunt. He took another sip of scotch and leaned against the bar. There wasn't anything remotely civilized about being terrorized by some sicko who got his kicks from frightening women. Every time he thought of how close he had been when that creep had... He bit back an oath and tightened his fingers around the glass. Whatever it took, he intended to make sure the guy never got another chance at Clea.

"And what have the police come up with so far?" Maggie argued, her Irish temper showing. "I'll tell you what they've come up with. Nothing."

"She does have a point," James added. "It doesn't look like Chicago's finest are getting anywhere fast on this case."

"And you're not going to be safe until that madman who attacked you is caught and locked behind bars," Maggie chimed in. "And the only way that's going to happen is if you have a professional, someone who knows how to hunt down that kind of vermin."

"I already have an entire *group* of professionals looking for him," Clea pointed out. "They're called the Chicago Police Department."

Maggie sighed. "I have the utmost respect for our police officers, but I'm afraid in this case, you just can't afford to rely on them to find that creature. Things are not the way they used to be when my father and brothers were on the force. Back then, the police would have had that...that cretin in custody right after you received the first letter.

"But things are different now. Now a police officer has to be concerned about things like overtime and budgets, instead of just making sure the streets are safe and the criminals are behind bars. There's not enough time or money to spend on real police work anymore. Why do you think so many officers are leaving the force? Why I wouldn't be a bit surprised if it's the reason both Ryan and his brother Connor decided to get out."

His aunt's little speech brought Ryan up short, reminding him that his departure from the LAPD two months ago marked the first time in four generations that no Fitzpatrick was serving in law enforcement somewhere. Of course, there was always the chance that wherever Connor was, he'd gone back to being a cop. For the life of him, he couldn't imagine his oldest brother doing anything else. But then, he'd never been able to imagine his father and brother nearly coming to blows five years ago, or the angry silence that had followed since Connor had packed up his things and left town.

"Maggie, I understand everything you're saying, and I appreciate what you're trying to do. But, I've made up my mind on this. It's bad enough I have to deal with the police poking their noses into my personal life. I refuse to have someone else snooping around in my affairs and watching my every move."

At the sharpness in Clea's tone, Ryan brought his wandering thoughts back to the present. The look she leveled at him probably made most men shiver, he decided. Fortunately, he didn't have an aversion to cold—not when he knew there was heat banked just below the surface of that frosty disdain of hers. And he intended to sample that heat again, he promised himself.

Clea picked up her coffee cup, then set it down again untouched. "I'm sorry to have wasted your time, Mr. Fitzpatrick. But I won't be needing your services after all."

So, they were back to Mr. Fitzpatrick. "No need to apologize, Duchess. I'm being compensated for my time." Pushing away from the bar, Ryan ambled over to the couch where Clea sat looking cool and regal in her ivory cocktail dress and pearls. He could still spot the nerves she was trying so hard to hide. She was scared down to her pretty little toes, and just didn't want to admit it.

He snagged an oatmeal cookie from the tray in front of her and devoured it in two bites. Taking his time, he skimmed his gaze over her face, down her body and back up again. "Besides," he said, reaching for another cookie. "The fringe benefits have certainly been worth it."

Her eyes snapped with green fire, anger overriding the fear, just as he had hoped it would. Suppressing a grin, he held up another cookie and said, "Great cookies."

"Thank you, dear," Aunt Maggie said from behind him.

He nodded, but held Clea's gaze. "So, you want me to follow you home, or are you going to stay here tonight?"

"Maybe I didn't make myself clear. Your assignment where I'm concerned is over."

"Oh, you made yourself perfectly clear." He polished off another cookie, then dusted his hands. "But you're not the one giving the orders. Aunt Maggie is. She's the one who hired me."

Clea's hands tightened into fists, but her voice remained surprisingly even as she said, "Well, I'm unhiring you. Consider yourself fired, Mr. Fitzpatrick."

Ryan merely smiled. "Afraid it doesn't work that way, Duchess. Since you didn't hire me, you can't fire me."

"Maggie, I'd appreciate it if you would explain to your nephew that his assignment, or whatever it is he chooses to call spying on me, is over."

"Ryan, you stick to her like glue until that…that man is caught and thrown into jail."

"Yes, ma'am."

"Maggie!" Clea protested.

Despite her fragile appearance, Margaret Fitzpatrick Donatelli was anything but, Ryan mused. Clea Mason was another story. She projected as tough, fearless. And her expression and voice gave no indication of the tangle of nerves working inside her. But she didn't seem able to keep her hands still. Right now they were gripping the cup of iced coffee she had picked up again, but had yet to taste. She was strong, determined, not used to relying on anyone. He had learned that within days of meeting her. But he suspected that Clea Mason wasn't half as tough as she pretended to be, or as she wanted everyone to think she was. An urge itched at him—to take her into his arms, hold her

and promise to keep her safe. But if he followed through
on that urge, she would probably sock him in his gut.

"Enough arguing, Clea. If your family was here, they'd
insist you get some sort of protection. But since they're not
here, it's up to us to see that you do. You're still welcome
to move in here—"

"Maggie, I can't. I'm not going to let him run me out
of my home."

"I understand. But until the police find that man, Ryan
will make sure you're safe."

Clea released a frustrated sigh and turned to Ryan's uncle. "James, please talk to your wife. Tell her this isn't
necessary."

James shook his head. "If there's one thing I've learned
in thirty years of marriage to Maggie, it's that once she
makes up her mind about something, there's no changing
it. Besides, she's right, Clea. We don't want anything to
happen to you."

"Come on, Duchess. How bad can it be to have me
around for a while?"

She arched her eyebrow in that regal way and somehow
managed to look down her pretty, straight nose at him, even
though he was the one standing. "You don't really want
me to answer that, do you?"

"Ouch!" With her wary green eyes and that smooth
black hair framing her face, she reminded him of a beautiful, sleek kitten—with very sharp claws. "Since I'm not
sure my poor ego can handle the answer, I'll just pass on
it for now."

"Wise decision."

Ryan eased onto the arm of the couch and caught a whiff
of her scent. Roses...and something exotic and elusive—
like her. He couldn't help wondering if her skin was as
petal-soft as it looked. Realizing the dangerous direction of
his thoughts, he dragged himself back to the problem at

hand. Finding Clea's sick fan. "But I do have a few other questions that I'd like to have answered."

She narrowed her eyes. "What kind of questions?"

"Oh, just routine stuff about the letters and calls you've been getting."

"I've already told the police everything."

"Yeah, I know. But I'd like you to tell it again—to me."

"Why should I?"

"Because I need as much information as you can give me so I can catch this guy. And I am going to catch him, Clea. You can bank on it. It would just be a lot easier if I had a little more to go on."

Some of the tension went out of her, and he could see the fatigue setting in. "All right," she said, her voice weary. "What do you want to know?"

Fifteen minutes later, in the privacy of his uncle's study, Ryan still had little or nothing more to go on. Frustrated, he ran a hand through his hair. "What about boyfriends?"

"I date men, Mr. Fitzpatrick. Not boys."

"Ryan," he corrected. "Then what about your *men* friends?"

"What about them?"

"Are you seeing anyone in particular right now?"

She stiffened, clearly uncomfortable. "Is that really any of your business?"

"Everything about you is my business. Now, how about the names of those men?"

"I'm not seeing anyone at the moment."

And if things worked out as he planned, the only man she'd be seeing in the near future would be him. "What about the last guy...uh, man friend?"

"What about him?"

"For starters, his name."

"Andrew."

Ryan wrote the name down in his book and waited.

When she said nothing more, he looked up from his pad. "Does Andy have a last name?"

"Davidson. And it's Andrew. No one calls him Andy."

"Figures," Ryan muttered as he jotted the name down. "When was the last time you saw Andrew?"

Clea paused. "It's been a while."

"Define 'a while' for me."

"Two years," she said, the words little more than a whisper.

"Two years?" he repeated, lifting his eyes up to meet hers. "You expect me to believe you haven't been involved with anyone for the past two years?"

"I don't care what you believe. You asked me a question and I've answered it. If you don't like the answer, then that's your problem."

"I didn't say I didn't like the answer. But we're being honest here. You've got a mirror. You don't need me to tell you that you're a beautiful, sexy and desirable woman because you already know it. Which means you're either lying, or the men in this town are all blind."

"Gee. You really have a way with compliments, Fitzpatrick. It's enough to turn a woman's head."

Ryan let her sarcasm roll right off him. "I call them like I see them. So which is it? Are you a liar, or are the men around here blind?"

"Neither. I haven't been interested and neither have they."

Ryan paused, curious about her reply. "How come?"

"How come what?"

"How come you haven't been in a romantic relationship for more than two years?"

"Because I haven't wanted to be in one. All right?" She made an exasperated sound. "Look—Destinations and its success is a high priority in my life. The bookings have more than doubled in the past six months. That means my workload has doubled, too."

At the arch of his eyebrow, she continued. "Listen, I'm not saying I'm the only one who's been putting in a lot of hours. Everyone's been working hard. But the corporate travel program is my baby. I intend to make it a success."

"And success means spending all of your time planning overpriced travel packages."

"I spend a *lot* of my time creating profitable sales packages. I'm also responsible for managing the agency and its operations. Which means researching and selecting a new computer system to handle the increased client base created by those expensive travel packages I design. I also hire all the new agents and make sure everyone is trained on the new equipment. So, yes, I guess I've allowed Destinations to take up a lot of my time lately, which means I haven't had much time to worry about whether or not I'm dating enough."

"Trust me, you're not. Haven't you ever heard that saying about 'all work and no play'?" he asked, pleased and at the same time disturbed at the workaholic life-style she had just described.

"I didn't say I haven't gone out with anyone for the past two years. I said I haven't been involved in a serious relationship for two years."

"Want to explain the difference to me?"

"The difference is that I can go out to dinner, the ballet or a charity event with a man without being emotionally involved with him."

"What about physically involved?"

He could practically see the steam rising from her on that one. "I'm not even going to answer that."

But she already had. *No lovers,* he concluded, more than a little pleased. "So who are these men you go to dinner, the ballet and charity things with?"

"Friends."

Ryan sighed. Getting answers from her was like pulling teeth. "Names, Duchess. I need names. No matter how remote they may seem to you, anyone you've gone out with or come into contact with could be the man we're looking for.''

Her hands curled into fists and she looked at him scornfully as she said, ''Patrick Evans, Donald Markson, Harry Peters. And stop calling me Duchess!''

''Anyone else?''

''Your uncle. I believe he escorted me to a black-tie fund-raiser where the agency was donating a cruise when your aunt was out of town about two months ago.''

He added his uncle's name to the list.

''You're putting James's name down on that list?''

''He's a man.''

''He's your uncle.'' Furious, she shot to her feet. ''This is crazy. You're crazy. None of those men are even capable of doing anything like this.''

''How do you know?''

''Because I know.'' She reached for the brandy he'd poured her earlier, swirled it around in her glass.

''You'd be surprised what a man will do when he finds himself obsessed with a woman.'' What disturbed him was that after kissing her and sampling that sweet heat of hers himself, he could almost understand a man being driven mad with the need for more of her.

''Not them. I told you, those men are my friends.''

''How about defining friend for me.''

''Just what the word implies—a friend, a companion, a pal.''

''Any of those pals ever graduate to being your lover?''

She slammed the glass down onto the table. ''No,'' she said, her voice like chipped ice.

''Any of them want to be?''

''That's it! I'm not listening to any more of this. You're just trying to embarrass me.''

Ryan caught her by the arm before she could storm off. ''What I'm trying to do is find out if the guy who's after you could be a former lover, or someone who wanted to be your lover, that might have gone nutso when you rejected him.''

''I haven't rejected anyone.''

''You rejected me,'' he reminded her.

Clea blinked. ''I— That was different.''

''How? I haven't made any secret of the fact that I'm attracted to you. I've asked you out several times. I've kissed you, and I've even asked you to marry me.''

''You weren't serious.''

''How do you know?'' Her scent reached out to him, tangled around him. Still holding her wrist, he rubbed his thumb across her pulse, felt the rapid beat beneath that smooth, soft skin.

''Because…because you're not,'' she told him, defiance and desire in her eyes as she looked at him. ''Men like you aren't interested in marriage.''

''What if I was?'' Desire licked through him. He lowered his head a fraction, until his mouth hovered just above hers. ''What if I told you I wanted you the first time I laid eyes on you? That I decided right then and there that we would be lovers. What if I told you that I thought there was a chance we might even work ourselves right up to marriage and a half-dozen kids?''

Shock—and something else—flashed across her face for a moment, and then she made her expression go blank. ''Then, I'd say you really are crazy because that isn't going to happen.'' She pushed against his chest.

Reluctantly, Ryan released her. He rubbed a hand down his face. She was right. He was crazy. Crazy not to realize that a woman who had avoided involvements for two years would run like a rabbit at the mention of anything sounding remotely like a relationship. And why in the devil had he said that stuff about marriage and kids?

''If you're finished with this third degree, I'd really like to go home.''

"All right. We'll call it quits for tonight." Ryan picked up his pad and pen, jammed them into the back pocket of his jeans. "We'll finish up in the morning."

Clea didn't say anything, didn't even spare him a parting glance. And even though she walked out of the study, Ryan couldn't shake the feeling that she was running scared, not from her sick admirer, but from him.

Clea slumped against the closed door of the study. She squeezed her eyes shut a moment, trying to cut off the emotions Ryan stirred up inside her. She didn't like feeling this way—scared, needy, wanting. It had been a long time since she'd experienced that tug of desire for a man. She didn't like feeling it for Ryan now. An old ghost of pain, dulled by time, wrapped around her heart, reminding her of that piece of herself that she'd lost so long ago because of her foolish choices.

She opened her eyes at the sound of footsteps near the door, and started down the hall. She had worked too hard putting her life back together again, she reminded herself. She wouldn't let some crazy attraction for Ryan Fitzpatrick jeopardize it now.

"You and Ryan all finished?" Maggie asked as Clea entered the living room moments later.

"Yes."

"We're finished for now," Ryan answered from behind her.

As far as she was concerned, they were finished. Period. Feeling more in control, Clea walked over to where Maggie was placing a fresh tray of coffee and snacks on the polished wood table. "I want you to know that I really appreciate everything you've done for me. Both of you," she added with a glance at James.

"I just wish we had been able to do more."

"You did too much as it is," Clea told her, her heart

swelling with affection. She kissed the older woman's cheek. "And I'm sorry for coming so unglued tonight."

"It was perfectly understandable. You had every reason to be afraid," Maggie told her.

"I'm just glad we were there," James added.

"Me, too," Clea said, remembering how frightened she'd been, and the relief that had washed over her when she'd seen Ryan's stern face, fire and determination burning in his eyes, as he'd battled through the crowd to reach her.

Glancing up, her pulse raced as she found his eyes fixed on her again. Only now, there was a different type of fire burning in them. Desire. She recognized it because an answering heat flowed through her veins. She jerked her gaze away. "It's really late. I need to be getting home."

"You sure we can't persuade you to spend the night?" Maggie asked.

"Thanks, but I think I'd really just like to go home." She walked over to the table near the doorway and picked up her evening bag.

"You know, staying with a friend or even going away for a while until this guy is caught might not be such a bad idea," Ryan offered as he swiped a fresh cookie from the newly filled tray his aunt had placed on the table.

"That's not an option," she told him, but wished that it were.

"Why not?"

"I have a job…responsibilities. I can't just walk away from them."

"No one's asking you to. Just take a little vacation somewhere for a couple of weeks," Ryan suggested. "I'm sure Aunt Maggie and Uncle James will understand."

"Of course, we'd understand," Maggie said. "In fact, we should have suggested it. Maybe you'd like to go visit one of your sisters or have them come see you."

The idea was more than a little tempting. But Lorelei and Desiree both had husbands now, and Lorelei was expecting a baby. She couldn't burden them with this. "No," Clea said, feeling suddenly lonely. "I don't really want a vacation now. And while I may have been frightened tonight, I refuse to let some creep make me run away and hide."

"There's a difference between running away and being smart."

"I'm smart enough to know that if I run away now because some jerk gets his jollies by scaring me, then he wins and I lose. I don't like losing." She'd worked too hard getting the corporate travel program under way to walk away now when it was coming to fruition. Just as she'd worked too hard at picking up the pieces of her life and putting it back together to risk losing it by falling for Ryan.

"He did more than scare you with a letter and phone call tonight," Ryan pointed out.

A chill spread over Clea, and she fought back a shudder of revulsion. She swallowed hard, refusing to let fear take hold of her again. "Thanks for the reminder. But I'll depend on the police and you to see that he doesn't get that close again. That is, if you think you can do the job."

"Don't worry. I'll find him," he told her, her sarcasm obviously not bothering him.

"I certainly hope so. For my sake."

James took her hands into his and studied her face closely. "You sure you'll be okay?" he asked, oblivious to the tension between her and his nephew.

"Yes, I'm sure," she assured him. "Thanks again for everything." She kissed his cheek and then Maggie's.

"I'm heading out, too." Ryan extended his hand to his uncle and gave his aunt a peck on her cheek before opening the door. "I'll be in touch."

She stepped outside and realized the temperature had dipped a good fifteen degrees since she had gone to dinner that evening. But the air seemed to hum with heat as Ryan followed her down the stairs.

"Cold?" Ryan asked when she hugged her arms about herself.

"A little," she admitted, picking up her pace as she headed down the street to where she had parked her car earlier that evening. She fumbled with her car keys, eager to put some distance between them.

"Here, let me get that for you."

"I can manage," she said and promptly dropped the keys.

Ryan swiped them up. "You really should reconsider staying at a friend's place for a while or having someone stay with you."

"I appreciate the advice. But I think I'll pass," she told him, holding out her hand for her car keys.

He brushed a strand of hair away from her mouth. "It wasn't exactly a suggestion."

"And I don't take orders from you," she told him, her heart pumping harder. "Give me my keys," she demanded, irritated by his high-handed manner, but even more by her response to his touch.

Ignoring her, Ryan pressed the remote button on her key chain. The lights went on inside the car and the door locks snicked open. He pulled open the car door.

She slid into her seat at once and fastened her seat belt, then held out her hand. "My keys."

He reached inside, his head dipping close to hers, inserted the key into the ignition and turned it. The engine of her pristine sedan purred to life, but Ryan made no effort to move.

The confines of the front seat seemed impossibly small and intimate with his head ducked close to hers, crowding her space. She had been chilly only moments before, but now she felt far too warm. "Was there something else you wanted?"

A slow smile spread across his lips. "As a matter of fact there is."

Clea hissed out a breath, chagrined that she'd left herself wide open for that one. "I'm tired, Fitzpatrick. So why don't you go ahead and get your juvenile come-on out of the way, then get out of my face so I can go home."

"You have such a suspicious mind, Duchess," he countered. "See that little honey of a car parked in front of you?"

Clea noted the vintage candy-apple-red convertible that was practically touching her front bumper. "Yes. I see it."

"It's mine," he told her, pride in his voice.

It figures, she thought. He had crowded her with his car just as he was crowding her with his handsome face and broad shoulders. "Congratulations. I hope you'll both be happy."

"I don't know what it is, but I just love that smart mouth of yours," he said, his gaze dropping to her lips.

Clea's pulse kicked into third gear at the hungry gleam in his eyes. She looked away. "Is there a point to this conversation?" she asked with as much sarcasm as she could muster, given the fact that her nerves were jumping like grasshoppers on a spring day. "In case you haven't noticed, it's really late, and I'd like to go home—which is a little difficult with your face stuck in front of my windshield."

"The point is, I'll be right behind you, and I want you to make sure you keep my car in sight in your rearview mirror until we get home."

Clea glared at him. "We? What do you mean until we get home? I'm going home. If you want to follow me there, fine. Go ahead. But afterwards, you go."

"One more thing, don't get nervous if you see a black Jeep parked in front of your place. I called Sean. He's bringing me a change of clothes and a razor," he said, then slammed the car door in her face and started to walk off.

Shutting off the car's engine, Clea unsnapped her seat belt and charged after him. "Get back here, Fitzpatrick.

What do you mean Sean's meeting you at my place with clothes? What do you need clothes for?''

He shot her that devilish smile. "I don't, but I thought you'd insist. I'll call Sean and tell him to forget the clothes.''

Furious with him, and with herself for stepping right into that one, Clea grabbed his arm to stop him from getting in his car. "Don't make me kill you, Fitzpatrick.''

"Problem, Duchess?'' he asked, his deep voice whisper-soft as it stroked over her nerve endings like a caress.

An autumn moon hung like a lantern in the night sky, illuminating the shock of black hair that fell across his brow. In the glow of the streetlamp, she could make out the shadow of whiskers along his sharp-edged jaw. His unsmiling mouth looked beautiful and inviting in that chiseled masculine face. He smelled like winter rain and pine forests, Clea thought as she lifted her gaze up to his. His blue eyes glistened dark and determined as he stared down at her. Her nervous stomach clenched and unclenched and she felt that warm tug of desire rippling through her again.

Suddenly, realizing how close they were, she dropped her hand. "I've changed my mind about this protection business. I don't care what Maggie and James say, I don't want you.''

"You sure about that?''

"Positive,'' she tossed back. It was bad enough the man made her hormones act up. The last thing she needed was to have him trailing her back to her apartment, sticking himself into her life. Especially when she was a jumble of nerves and emotions.

He reached out and tucked a strand of hair behind her ear. Her pulse skittered at the intimate gesture, but she refused to retreat. As though sensing her reaction, his mouth curved in that familiar smile. "That's too bad. Your not wanting me, I mean. It would have made us being roommates a lot more interesting.''

"Roommates?" she repeated. "We're not going to be roommates."

"Sure we are. Because from now on, Duchess, wherever you go, I go. That's what a bodyguard does."

Three

___

"A bodyguard!"

"That's right," Ryan informed her.

Clea jerked away from him. "No way," she fired off, reminding him of his five-year-old godchild.

Damn, Ryan thought. She was so distressed that he almost felt sorry for her. Almost, but not quite. Not enough for him to risk leaving her unprotected. "I'm afraid you don't have a choice."

She stiffened with indignation. "Wrong. I *do* have a choice," she told him, her eyes shooting off angry green sparks. "And I choose *not* to have a bodyguard. I don't need one, and I certainly don't need *you.*"

"Oh, you need me all right. You're just too stubborn to admit it."

"Why, you—"

He caught her by the shoulders. "Wake up and smell the coffee, Clea," he said, his voice harsh because he needed for her to see reason. "I've made light of what's happened tonight because I wanted to wipe that terrified look out of your eyes. I can see how that was a mistake. Because this isn't a game. You're in danger. There's some crazy out there stalking you. Or have you forgotten that fact?''

"Believe me, that's something I'm not likely to forget.'' She balled her hands into fists, propped them on her hips, faced him eye to eye, toe to toe. "There's hardly an hour that goes by that I'm not aware of it. I think about it when I open my eyes in the morning and when I close them at night. I think about it every time the telephone rings or a letter shows up in my mail. So, don't you stand there and tell me I'm not taking this seriously. Because I am.''

"Then quit fighting me and let me do what I'm being paid to do,'' Ryan told her.

"Which is what? Trying to get into my pants?''

Ryan flushed, knowing there was some truth in what she said. "I haven't made a secret of the fact that I want you. But that's personal, and you and I will deal with that when this is over. You don't have to worry about it getting in the way of me doing my job—which is to keep you safe from that creep who grabbed you tonight.''

"And, of course, since you're an ace private eye for all of a...what is it now, a month? I'm supposed to put my trust in your vast experience?''

"I'd say the fact that I was a cop for twelve years counts for something. If nothing else it should inspire some confidence that I know what I'm doing.''

"Well, it doesn't. Why should I believe you can find this guy when the police who've been working on this for months can't?''

"Because I promise you that I will find him and stop him.''

"Fine. You go right ahead and play super sleuth. But you'll to do it without playing bodyguard to my helpless female. Forget it, Fitzpatrick. I don't need you to protect me.''

Lord, but the woman was stubborn, Ryan thought, his patience wearing thin. "Because you can take care of yourself. Right?"

"That's right. I can."

"And if your admirer decides to cop another feel like he did tonight, how do you plan to handle that? By screaming bloody murder again?"

Clea sucked in a breath. "That won't happen again. I'll be more careful in the future," she told him, her voice suddenly tight.

Hating himself for putting that haunted look back in her eyes, Ryan smacked his hand against the car door. "Dammit, Clea."

"Don't you swear at me, Fitzpatrick," she fired back, some of the steel returning to her voice.

He raked at his hair. "Do you really expect me to just leave you alone so that sicko can take another shot at you?"

"You're a private investigator. I expect you to investigate. Track down where his calls are coming from. Or do some kind of computer search. Or...or whatever it is you do to find a suspect. Just find out who's doing this to me and make him stop."

"I'll hop right to it, Duchess," he countered, not bothering to mask his sarcasm. Did she really think it was that easy to find a clever criminal who didn't want to be caught? "Any other orders?"

Her lips thinned at the nickname. "Just do your job, and let *me* worry about my safety."

Ryan caught her by the wrist as she turned to leave. "And just how do you plan to do that? How do you plan to protect yourself until he's caught? By putting new locks on your doors and windows? By making sure you're not caught in any more crowds?" He didn't give her a chance to respond. "Or did you plan to continue with business as usual, but watch over your shoulder every time you go somewhere and hope you'll be able to spot him if he's following you? Or maybe…just maybe, you can have the flight attendant check out the identity of the man seated next to you on an airplane. And the usher check out who's sitting behind you in the theater. And the restaurant manager give you a bio on the guy seated at the next table. Or—''

"Stop it," she cried out, pulling free from his grasp. "You're just trying to scare me."

"You're damn right I'm trying to scare you. You should be scared," he told her in a voice that had made the men under his command shudder. But not Clea. No, the lady didn't even flinch.

"This isn't a game, Clea," he said growing more frustrated by the second. "I've seen nuts like this before. The fellow who's been sending you those notes and calling you on the phone upped the ante tonight. If he risked being seen, risked getting caught, it's because the sick thrill he gets from scaring you with letters and calls isn't enough any longer. He wants more. And, believe me, he isn't going to stop until he gets it. Until he gets *you*. The best chance you've got of stopping him is for me to get him first."

He had to give her credit. She didn't wince, didn't break into hysterics, didn't start crying like a lot of women would do. But despite her brave front, she was scared. He could see it in her eyes, in the way she clenched and unclenched the car keys in her fist. He could feel it in the air between them. Yet her gaze remained steady, her voice even, as she said, "Give me one reason I should believe you'll be any more successful at finding him than the police have been?"

"I'll give you three. First," he said, ticking off his index finger, "unlike the cops, I only have one case to work on solving. This one. Second," he said, holding up another digit, "you've got good men assigned to your case, but I'm better. I've got twelve years' experience as a cop and believe me, I was damned good at my job. And third," he finished, marking off another finger, "while the police might try, they don't have a vested interest in seeing that nothing happens to you. I, on the other hand, do. Because when this is over, you and I are going to explore getting a whole lot closer.''

''I'm not even going to bother arguing with you about that ridiculous statement.''

Ryan watched her hook a loose strand of hair behind her ear, and eye him warily. He found himself amused by the nervous feminine gesture that was so unlike Clea. With her swath of black hair, green eyes and sharp tongue, she reminded him of a feisty kitten, hissing and swiping with her claws even as she demanded that she be rubbed. He inched a bit closer.

''All right,'' she said, her voice grim. ''I don't seem to have much in the way of choices—not if I want to put an end to this nightmare. So, I'll agree to a bodyguard. But I have some conditions of my own.''

''Which are?''

''I pay Fitzpatrick Securities—not Maggie and James.''

''Done.''

At his easy acquiescence, she narrowed her eyes. ''Just how much is a bodyguard going to cost me?''

''Three-hundred-fifty a day, plus expenses.''

''That's robbery.''

''That's the discounted family rate. The usual fee is five hundred.''

She opened her mouth, shut it. ''I get the family rate.''

''Done. What else?''

''I want Sean or Michael, not you.''

Ryan grinned. ''Sorry, Duchess. That's not an option.''

''But, I—''

''Even if I were inclined to give you up, which I'm not, my brothers are tied up on other cases, and I'm not trusting this to an operative. So, you're stuck with me.''

''Stuck is right,'' she muttered.

''Come on. If you give me a chance, you'll find out I'm

really a nice guy. Want me to provide you with references?" he teased.

"From who? Your legion of lady friends?"

"Legion?" Ryan repeated, amused. "You overestimate my appeal to the fairer sex. Besides, there's only one woman I'm interested in," he said, skimming a finger along her soft cheek. "You."

Those forest-green eyes of hers darkened a moment. He spied the telltale quickening of the pulse at her neck. Then she shoved his hand aside. "Forget it, Fitzpatrick. I'm not buying."

"I wasn't aware I was selling anything," he told her, dogging her footsteps to her car.

She made a most unladylike snicker as he opened her door. "Oh, you're selling all right," she told him as she slid onto her seat and fastened her seat belt.

"Yeah?" he said, feigning innocence. He draped his arm over the top of the open door and admired the way the shoulder belt outlined her breasts.

"Yeah," she mimicked.

He dipped his head inside the car to see her face more clearly. "And just what is it you think I'm selling?"

"You and I both *know* what you're selling—a quick tumble on the sheets and promises of paradise in your arms."

Ryan nearly groaned at the images her words evoked. He was already aroused—a constant state, it seemed, whenever he was within five feet of the woman. And now he was as hard as a hammer and itching to take her in his arms. "I don't know about the quick part, but I sorta like the idea of us finding paradise together. I'm game, if you are."

She bristled. If she had been a cat, every hair on her back would be standing straight up, Ryan thought. Damn, if she didn't turn him on even with that schoolmarm scowl on her face.

"You needn't bother wasting that sexy little grin on me, Fitzpatrick," she told him in that prim voice. "I've told you before, I'm not interested."

"You sure about that?"

"Yes."

He traced a fingertip along her neck, watched surprise flicker across her face. Her pulse began another frantic dance. He saw her gaze drop to his mouth, her eyes darken to a green as deep as a magnolia leaf. Heat flooded his body, and Ryan moved a fraction closer, eager to sample her lips again, to taste all that sweet heat she kept locked up in the ice.

"Let's make sure," he whispered against her lips.

Clea's look moved up from his mouth to his eyes. She blinked. Were it not for the painful ache pressing against the zipper on his jeans, he would have laughed at her half horrified, half aroused expression. She pushed at his shoulders and Ryan stepped back. "I'm already sure," she told him, leveling him with a look as cold as a Minnesota winter.

"Why don't I see if I can change your mind?"

She yanked the door closed. "It'd be a waste of time because I won't," she told him and started the car.

"You wouldn't want to make a little wager on that, would you now?" he asked, wanting to see that fire darken her eyes again.

"I don't gamble," she told him, going all prickly just as he had known she would. "And if I were you, I wouldn't bet on me having a change of heart. Now get out of my way."

Ryan jumped back as she gunned the engine and took off down the street. "Oh, but I *am* betting on it," he said as he hopped into his convertible and took off after her. He zipped through a yellow light and whipped around a corner behind her white sedan. A smile tugged at his lips. "You might take me on one hell of a chase, Duchess," he murmured as she made another swift turn. "But make no mistake about it. I *am* going to catch you."

Oh, what a royal idiot you are, Clea Mason. She pulled the car to a stop in front of her condo. "A first-class, certifiable idiot," she muttered, reliving those moments outside the Donatellis'. She slammed the driver's door closed and walked around to the trunk of the car to retrieve the briefcase she had been in too much of a hurry to unpack before she had left for dinner.

How on earth could I have come so close to allowing Ryan to kiss me? Allow? She scoffed at that notion as she snatched the burgundy leather case, and headed up the sidewalk. She had been darn close to *demanding* that he kiss her. How was she going to convince him that she wasn't interested in an affair with him, if every time the man came within a mile of her, her traitorous body went wacko?

Irritated with herself, she absently collected her mail and stuffed the bundle into her briefcase before starting up the stairs. Maybe it was a hormonal thing, and a woman's libido just launched into overdrive once she passed thirty, Clea reasoned.

Right, she mocked silently. And if she bought that one, there were a whole slew of people waiting to sell her a couple dozen bridges. Hormones? she scoffed. Then how come not once in the past six years had any man even come close to revving up those hormones—let alone causing them to explode—until Ryan Fitzpatrick?

Because the men she dated were nothing like Ryan. Those men weren't pushy and arrogant and so all-fired sure of themselves. They were gentlemen. They were polite, refined. And as dull as dishwater, she admitted to herself. And not one of those men had ever made her blood spin or her pulse quicken with just a look, the way Ryan did. Not one of them had made her ache for the feel of his mouth, the touch of his hands on her body. Not one of them had ever tempted her and made her want more.

But Ryan did. The infernal man excited her even though she had sworn no man would ever have that power over her again. As much as she hated the fact, she was attracted to him.

Clea sighed. No point fooling herself. It was more than attraction and she knew it. She was drawn to him in a way she had never been drawn to any man before, and it scared the devil out of her. It wouldn't be so frightening if the attraction were just physical.

Oh, she liked his looks all right. That sassy dimple mixed in with those Viking cheekbones and to-die-for blue eyes were certainly reason enough to find him tempting. That gorgeous, toned body of his didn't hurt, either. But it was the whole package that intrigued her, tempted her, made her ache. The reckless charm and passion, the lusty way he seemed to enjoy life. The devotion to his family. And that mile-wide protective streak she had witnessed in him on more than one occasion was only one more check mark on the list of things that appealed to her.

The dratted man even liked children, she acknowledged, recalling how he had charmed her co-worker's toddler at the wedding reception last month. She could still see the delight on that little girl's face when Ryan had lifted her up into his arms and danced her around the room. He had been so kind, so gentle with the child's tender feelings.

Clea pressed a hand to her chest at that tight, achy feeling the memory stirred. Blast you, Ryan Fitzpatrick, for making me like you—for making me want what I can't have.

At the squeal of tires turning onto her street, Clea swiped at her eyes and hurriedly shoved her key into the lock. Pushing open the door to her apartment, she stepped inside, determined to shake thoughts of Ryan from her mind. She set down her briefcase and flipped on the light switch. Delicate beams of light spilled over the room, giving the ivory-colored carpet a champagne glow, and winking along the marble inset of the fireplace.

Her gaze skipped over some of the items that had turned the apartment into her home. A Monet reproduction of water lilies covering the far wall. The crystal vase of those same lilies in silk, given to her as a birthday gift by her sisters, that now sat atop a gleaming wood coffee table.

Setting down her evening purse, she walked into the picture-book perfect room she had created, and trailed her fingers along the length of the couch. The sage-colored damask fabric she had fallen in love with a year ago still looked and felt as lovely and elegant as the day she had forked over a full month's salary to buy it.

She had everything she wanted, Clea told herself. Her home was beautiful, serene. Not a thing was out of place. No man's dirty socks or sports magazines littered the floor. There were none of those annoying cigars she had witnessed Ryan smoking at the wedding, smelling up the place. And best of all, there was no Ryan here to argue and fight with her over what she should or shouldn't do. Everything was perfect. Just as it should be. Just as she wanted it to be.

Then why did it suddenly all feel so empty?

"If you ever decide to give up the travel business, you should consider taking a shot at the Indy 500."

Clea nearly jumped out of her skin at the sound of Ryan's voice. She whirled around and spied him standing in the doorway. And darned if her rebellious heart didn't pick up speed. In his oxford shirt, dark jeans, and wind-roughened hair, he should have looked shoddy, out-of-place in the elegant surroundings. He didn't. He looked wonderfully sexy and as though he were right where he belonged.

"Don't you believe in knocking?"

"Door was open," he informed her, her sarcasm obviously not fazing him. He shoved the door closed. "So, who in the devil taught you how to drive?"

"My father."

"Did he by chance mention anything about speed limits and slowing down for turns?"

Clea tossed up her chin. "My father was an excellent teacher," she told him, knowing full well that she'd been driving too fast, desperately trying to outrun the feelings he'd invoked in her.

"I'm sure he was. But tell me, did the poor fellow's hair turn white while he was teaching you? Or did he just give up and pull it out?" Ryan didn't bother waiting for an invitation, just waltzed right in as though he owned the place.

"I'll have you know, I've never gotten a ticket in my life and neither have my sisters. And Daddy taught all of us to drive." No point in mentioning anything about the female stunt-car driver on one of her parents' movie sets who had shown her and her sisters some fancier moves, she decided.

"Sisters?" He arched his brow. "Aunt Maggie mentioned that before. I didn't know you had any sisters," he said as he prowled the room, inspecting her paintings, skimming a finger over her favorite book of Yeats lying on the table.

"You don't have to sound so surprised," she told him, feeling far too vulnerable with him in her home, touching her things, watching her.

He shifted a glance up from the crystal frog he'd been studying. Awareness whispered between them as his eyes, those intense blue eyes of his, slid over her like a lover's touch. "I am surprised. I sort of had you pegged as an only child."

"Well, you were wrong. I have two sisters."

He wandered over to the mantel and picked up a photograph of her with her two siblings. The shot had been a favorite, taken the day the three of them celebrated her landing her first real job after graduation. She'd been on top of the world and so proud to have been offered a position with one of Chicago's top travel agencies. "This them?"

"Yes." Suddenly anxious for him to leave, Clea removed the framed snapshot from his hands to return it to the mantel. But she couldn't resist running her own fingertips over the images first. She'd been so sure of herself back then, so positive that her life would turn out exactly as she wanted it to, exactly as she planned for it to. Only she hadn't counted on falling for Eric Ramsey and ruining all those carefully made plans. But she'd made it through those dark times, put her life back together and started over, she reminded herself. She had plotted out a new course for her life—one that she intended to follow. And she refused to let Ryan mess it all up for her.

"They're very pretty."

"They're also very married," she said and nearly cringed at her waspish tone. Great! Just what his ego needed, she thought, noting the amusement dancing in his eyes. Now he would no doubt believe she was jealous. "What I meant was, that they're not available because they're married."

A grin flirted across his lips. "That's okay. You're the only Mason sister I'm interested in."

Changing the subject, she said, "Well, as you can see, I made it home safe and sound. So you can leave now." She walked across the room, opened the door.

To her relief, Ryan followed her without a word. Good, he was going. She needed to be alone, she told herself, to shore up her defenses against Ryan and this chemistry that seemed to be simmering between them.

He paused in front of her, removed her hand from the doorknob and gently shut the door. She braced herself, sure he was going to kiss her. But instead of kissing her, he dropped to his knees and began examining the lock. "What do you think you're doing?"

"I'd think that was obvious," he told her as he flicked the dead bolt closed, then opened it again. "I'm checking your locks."

"You don't need to do that. It's not necessary."

"Sure it is." He slammed the dead bolt home a second time, only to unlock it and try again. He shook his head and made that snickering sound so typical of a man whenever it came to anything mechanical—anything that a "little woman" couldn't possibly understand. He shook his head like a doctor about to deliver bad news, then stood. "What kind of an alarm system do you have?"

"I don't…have an alarm system, I mean."

Another of those snickering sounds followed, and before she could call him on it, he asked, "What about a security guard for this neighborhood?"

"There isn't one," she explained—to his back because he was already moving across the room and inspecting the locks on her windows.

He shook his head again, made more of those snicking sounds that Clea realized she detested. When he started down the hall toward her bedroom, she'd had enough. "All right. That's it." She blocked his path. "Just what do you think you're doing?"

"Checking out your security system or what little there is of it," he said dryly. But his lips curved ever so slightly in what looked suspiciously close to a smile.

"My security's just fine."

"Duchess, your security sucks."

Clea blinked. "I'll have you know that's a top-of-the-line dead bolt on that door," she said, stabbing her finger at the lock in question.

He snorted. "A ten-year-old could pick that lock and be inside here in five seconds flat."

"I don't have any ten-year-old lock pickers in my neighborhood," she shot back and earned another of those superior male noises. "Fine. If it'll make you go away, I'll agree to get a better lock. Tomorrow."

She tugged at his arm, intending to drag him to the door if she had to. Ryan didn't budge. Not a single step. The man had to weigh a ton and was as solid as a piece of granite—all six feet two inches of him. She gave up the impossible. She knew darned well she couldn't move a bull, so Clea marched over to the door. She yanked it open again. Squaring her shoulders, she hiked up her chin and in her frostiest tone, said, "I want you to leave. Now."

This time he didn't bother hiding the smile, and blast it if that dimple of his didn't wink at her. "We need to have a little talk, Duchess." Clamping his gaze on her face, he started toward her.

"I'm tired of talking," she informed him, nerves jumping, her heart thudding faster and harder the closer he came. "I want you to go."

He stopped so close to her that she could see flecks of black in his eyes, threads of silver in his hair. Instinctively, Clea retreated a step. A mistake, she realized when she found the door at her back and Ryan standing in front of her. He propped one arm up, rested his hand against the door. She could smell the autumn night and wind on him. And for one crazy moment she wondered whether she would be able to taste that night air on his oh-so-close lips. "I mean it, Fitzpatrick. I want you to leave."

Ignoring her, he dipped his head a fraction closer. Clea's heart stammered. She braced herself, both anticipating and fearing his kiss.

That devilish smile sneaked across his lips. "Afraid I'm going to have to disappoint you, then. Because I'm not going anywhere. I'm spending the night."

Four

"**A**bsolutely not." Tossing that stubborn chin of hers up a notch, Clea brushed past him and began pacing around the fancy couch. "You're not staying here."

"Be reasonable, Clea. I'm your bodyguard, and I—"

"I don't care if you're the King of England. Your staying here was not part of the deal. I'll put up with you following me when I leave here. But when I'm home, I want my privacy. So you do your bodyguarding from a distance."

"Maybe I should explain the term bodyguard for you," he said, his patience beginning to fray. "It means someone who guards and protects your body, your being, your life. To do that, it usually helps if the person you're trying to guard is at least within shouting distance."

"That's your problem, Fitzpatrick. Not mine. You want the job? Then you figure out a way to make it work. But you don't stay here."

Frustrated, his ego dented at her reluctance to be any-where near him, temper rumbled inside him. "And if your admirer decides to pay you a visit here. What then, Duchess? How do you propose I protect you if I'm down the block or twenty miles away?"

He saw the color drain out of her face. Way to go, Fitzpatrick. If charm and reasoning don't work, just scare her to death.

"He isn't going to come here," she said, her voice shaky despite her defiant stance.

"He came to the theater."

"Because he felt safe in the crowd. But he'd never risk coming here and being seen."

There was every reason to worry that the wacko would show up here for that very same reason—because he *had* been desperate enough to come after her at the theater tonight. And that's what bothered Ryan, made him push her when he probably shouldn't. Things had become more serious tonight. The stakes were higher. But now was not the time to share his suspicions with Clea—not when she was dead on her feet and, thanks to him, scared. Rubbing a hand over his face, Ryan mentally kicked himself again for adding to her distress. "You're probably right," he said, even though he didn't believe it.

"Of course, I am," she said with a bravado that didn't quite ring true.

"Yeah," he said, moving across the room to stand beside her. "I bet after that scream you let loose at the theater, the guy's probably hiding under a rock somewhere praying he gets his hearing back." And it had better be a big rock, Ryan added silently, because he intended to find the creep, and when he did, he'd make sure the man paid for every anxious, frightened moment he had caused Clea.

"You're a real funny man, aren't you?"

"Hey, I'm serious. My ears are still ringing from that squeal of yours. You've got a real set of lungs, Duchess."

Her lips hinted at a smile, just as he had hoped. He'd wanted to wipe away her edginess. He wanted her to trust him to keep her safe. "Then you don't think he'll come here?"

"Probably not," Ryan said, hoping it wasn't a lie. "But just to be on the safe side, I'm going to spend the night." He held up his hand before she could object again. "Downstairs in my car. I'll be right outside in front of your place, so you have nothing to worry about. Okay?"

She nodded.

Ryan tipped up her chin, brushed his thumb along her jaw. "Trust me. He's not going to get a second chance at you. To do that, he'd have to get through me. And I promise you, he *won't* get past me."

"I believe you," she whispered.

Her skin was softer than he'd remembered, her scent more alluring, Ryan thought as he stroked her velvety cheek. Courage and fear shone from those deep green eyes looking up at him. Steel and silk. A heady combination in a woman. A man could live a lifetime searching for a woman like this. And she had a way of looking at a man that could make him sweat, make him burn with wanting.

Desire fisted in his gut, heated his blood as he continued to look at her and want. He wanted to taste her again now, to see if she was everything he remembered. And because he wanted it so badly, because he was just short of needing that kiss the way some men need a drink, he dropped his hand and turned away from her. Ryan fought against the ache inside him, as his brother's warning came back to him in a rush.

We both know becoming involved with a client screws up your judgment. You lose focus because you're no longer thinking with just your head. If that happens on this case, it's Clea who's going to pay the price.

Michael had been right. He couldn't afford to lose focus by letting his feelings for Clea get in the way of his doing his job. The fact that he had come very close to doing just that irritated him as much as it confused him. He'd never lost sight of his responsibilities before. Never once as a cop had he lost focus on what needed to be done. He wouldn't do so now, he vowed. It was his responsibility to keep Clea safe and find the creep who was after her. Afterward, when this mess was over with, he would sort out his feelings for her.

But now…now he needed to do his job. Feeling somewhat more in control, Ryan turned around. He cut a glance to the fancy couch where she stood, but opted instead for a big cushy-looking chair next to it. "What time do you get up in the morning?"

She narrowed her eyes. "What kind of question is that?"

"Pretty straightforward, I thought," he said, noting the irritation in her voice and glad the charged moment between them had passed. "I'm an early riser myself."

"Bully for you."

"My guess is you are, too. Morning's usually a great time to—"

"So help me, Fitzpatrick, if this is another of your feeble attempts to get into my pants, I swear, I'll—"

"Whoa, Duchess." Ryan grinned. "As appealing as that idea is, I'm afraid we're going to have to put the fun stuff on hold. We've got other things that need taking care of first."

"There isn't going to be any 'fun' stuff," she assured him.

He decided it best not to argue the point now. "Assuming we're both early risers, I'd like us to get an early start in the morning."

A tiny wrinkle creased her brow. "An early start on what?"

"Finding out who's behind the letters and phone calls you've been getting. I've got a lot more questions that need answering."

"What type of questions?"

"For starters the name of any man you've come into contact with for, say, the last six months."

"What for?"

"To look for suspects."

"No one I know would do this to me."

"Then it shouldn't be a problem ruling them out as suspects. I want a list of names, Clea."

"Now?"

"The sooner the better. You want to wait until morning? That's fine by me. But I want those names."

"Do you have any idea how many people you're talking about? I run a travel agency, for pity's sake, and I'm the one behind the corporate travel program. Most of the clients I deal with are men. Which means I have contact with dozens of men. More, if I operate any of the tours myself."

"Then we'll start with the most obvious. I want the names of the men you deal with on a regular basis. Anyone you've worked with or socialized with in the past six months. Anyone you...." He paused when he noted that she hadn't moved so much as a muscle, but merely stared at him as though he were insane. "You might want to write some of this down."

She scowled at him, but marched over to her briefcase and withdrew what he surmised was a portable computer. She turned it on and began typing furiously. Her fingers moved swiftly and efficiently over the miniature keyboard, and Ryan couldn't help but wonder how those long, slender fingers would feel moving over his skin.

"What else?"

Ryan swallowed and returned to the list of notes he had made. "I'll need to see your appointment schedule for the past six months, and a copy of everything on your schedule for the coming month."

"Is that really necessary?"

"Until we find this guy, I want to know where you are and who you're with, every minute of every day."

She punched at some more keys. "Is that it?"

He nodded. "Except for the letters. I'll need to see those, too."

"I told you, I didn't keep them all. And the police have all of the others—except for the last three. I was supposed to bring them down to the station yesterday, but I got backed up at the office and never made it."

Ryan made a note to request copies of the earlier letters from the police in the morning. "You can give them to me. I'll see that the police get them."

"Now?"

"If you don't mind," he said with a smile.

"Oh, why on earth would I mind?" she asked, making no attempt to disguise her irritation. "After all, it's only past midnight, and I don't have to be at the office until eight in the morning. That means I can sleep a whole six and a half hours before getting up for work."

"Plenty of time. How about if I wake you with coffee and doughnuts? The jolt of caffeine and sugar should get you moving and into the office on time." He leaned back in the chair and stretched his arms up to clasp them behind his head.

"Please, do make yourself at home," she told him, her voice heavy with sarcasm.

"Thanks."

Setting the computer on the coffee table, she stood and stomped off down the hall.

Ryan chuckled as he watched the stiff line of her back disappear inside one of the rooms. Standing, he walked over to the table and looked at the little computer. Fancy and expensive. Just like its owner, he mused, noting the neat list of items she had posted under her "To Do" list for the next day.

"Here you are," she said moments later as she tossed him the small packet of letters. "Enjoy yourself."

He doubted that he would, Ryan thought as he studied

one of the meticulously hand-printed envelopes. He doubted the guy had left any prints, but took care withdrawing the note inside. He had barely finished the first paragraph before a foul taste filled his mouth. Deciding to read them later when he was alone, he returned the letter to its envelope and dropped the bundle into an evidence bag. "All of them as bad as that last one?" he asked.

"No. At first they weren't quite as explicit. The last few seemed to be a little worse."

A little more twisted, Ryan corrected, but kept that opinion to himself. No wonder she freaked out at the theater, he thought. "You must be dead on your feet. Why don't we call it a night so you can get your beauty sleep."

"How considerate of you."

"That's me, Mr. Consideration." He wanted to reach out and touch her again. He stuffed his hands into his pockets instead. "I'll be posted outside. You won't be alone. Okay?"

"Okay."

"Good. Now come lock up behind me. Make sure you put the safety latch on and use the dead bolt," he told her as he started for the door.

"Yes, sir," she shot back with none of the respect her answer would imply.

"If I were you, I'd go straight to bed and get some rest because tomorrow's going to be busy. I'll need that list of names and those schedules first thing in the morning."

"You're very good at giving orders," she pointed out.

"And you don't like taking them," he noted with amusement.

"No, I don't."

"Like calling the shots, do you?"

"Yes."

He'd noticed. The lady was one cool, controlled number most of the time except when he got too close. Considering the fact that she managed to knock him off balance without even trying, he liked knowing that he could rattle her, too. "Well, Duchess, until we find this admirer of yours, I'm afraid you're going to have to trust me to call the shots as I see them."

She propped her fists on her hips. "And if I don't?"

"You willing to take that chance?"

She didn't like it. He could see it in the set of her chin, in the fury flashing in her eyes. "I'll listen to what you have to say, and then *I* decide whether or not to go along with it."

"That's not an option. You follow the precautions I set out for you or—"

"Don't push me, Fitzpatrick. I don't like being pushed."

"And I don't like prima donnas who are too stubborn to do what they should for their own good."

"Tough! I don't like macho detectives who think a woman is supposed to obey their every command. I've got news for you, pal. You push me too far," she said, poking a finger against his chest, "and I push back. Don't forget yours isn't the only private detective agency in this town."

Ryan looked down at the finger pressed against his chest. "That a threat, Duchess?"

"A warning, Fitzpatrick." She dropped her hand. "Now that we understand one another and you've finished issuing your list of demands, I'd like you to leave so I can go to bed." She started to yank open the door.

Ryan slapped it shut before she had managed to open it more than a foot. "I'm not finished with my demands yet," he told her, edging closer until her back was pressed against the door. "There's one more thing that I want."

"What?" she asked, the word a throaty whisper that licked over his skin and made his blood go from simmer to boil.

"This." His mouth crashed down on hers. He kissed her hard, deep, fast, with all the hunger that had been building inside him for months. With all the need that had been growing since that first taste of her at the wedding.

She parted her lips and he drove deeper still. Her lips were softer than he had remembered, the taste of her sweeter. And he didn't seem able to get enough. When her tongue tangled with his, he groaned. He could feel himself sinking, sinking, sinking. He should stop now, he told himself. He was in dangerous water here, and it was getting more dangerous by the second. And he wasn't sure he could remember how to swim, wasn't sure he even wanted to save himself if drowning in her kisses felt this good.

Just as he was ready to go under for the third time, the arms that had been twined tightly around his neck pushed against his chest until he eased his hold. When she pulled her mouth free, he reached for her again.

"Ryan, no. Wait," she said, her voice a ragged whisper. "Your beeper. Your beeper's going off."

His eyes blurry, his breath shallow, he tried to focus on what she was saying.

"Your beeper," she repeated. "It's been going off for the past couple of minutes."

Gradually, as his vision cleared and the blood storming in his ears settled to a roar, Ryan looked down at the black gadget attached to his belt. He hit the shut-off switch and glanced at the message displayed. The numbers 9-1-1 flashed in red, the agency code for an emergency, and were followed by his backup's code. He swore. His entire body went on full alert. "I've got to go."

"What is it? What's wrong?"

"No time to explain now. Just lock the door and go to bed. I'll see you in the morning."

He was gone, Clea realized the next morning as she scanned the street in search of the red convertible that had remained parked outside her apartment throughout the night. After Ryan's brief phone call to let her know everything was okay, she had finally done as he had asked, and gone to bed. Not that it had done her much good. Sleep had come in bits and pieces, sandwiched between nightmares of what had happened at the theater and dreams of running to the safety of Ryan's arms.

And each time she had awakened feeling alone and wanting, she'd wandered to the window. He'd been there every time, sitting in his car or leaning against it. No one had relieved him as she had expected. He'd kept the watch himself. More than once she'd been tempted to tell him to go home, but had shied away from doing so. In part, because she felt safer knowing he was there. And in part, she admitted as she touched her lips, because the memory of the kiss they'd shared was still too fresh in her mind. She'd wanted more time, more distance, to pull the reins in on the feelings he'd awakened inside her.

Well, she had gotten her wish. She stared at the large blond male at the wheel of the sedate, black sedan now parked where Ryan had been. An odd sense of abandonment settled over her as she released the bedroom curtain and went to finish dressing.

She should be grateful that he was gone, and that she wouldn't have to face him this morning, Clea told herself a few minutes later. Picking up a brush, she dragged it through her hair. Just as she should be grateful that his beeper had interrupted them when it had last night.

Last night. Clea tossed down the brush and squeezed her eyes shut. If asked, she would have sworn she had known desire before last night, that she had understood the gentle yearning caused by it. But nothing...*nothing* had come close to preparing her for that frantic rush of need that had exploded inside her when Ryan had kissed her.

She pressed her fingers to her belly, recalling the sweet, wild ache that had fired through her when his mouth had latched onto hers, so hot, so hungry. Desire had ignited in her like a match to dry tinder, and within seconds that spark had escalated to a fast-burning, out-of-control blaze. She'd opened to him, wrapped her arms and herself around him, wanting, needing, demanding more.

Never had she experienced passion so intense. Passion that overwhelmed her, consumed her, made her forget all reason, made her forget all the careful plans and promises she'd made to herself. And no doubt it had been unfulfilled passion that had played a role in her restless night. Because each time she had closed her eyes, she had seen Ryan's face again, had felt his mouth on her skin and his hands on her body.

Clea snapped open her eyes, to shut off the erotic memories. She sucked in a breath and stared at her image in the mirror. Frowning at the telltale shadows beneath her eyes, she dabbed on a bit more concealer. "I *am* glad things stopped when they did," she told her reflection. There was no place in her life for that kind of passion. There was no place in her life for Ryan, she reminded herself. He didn't fit in with her plans, and she could never...would never fit into his.

The doorbell rang, interrupting her thoughts. Quickly, Clea snatch up the bright red and green scarf. Draping it across one shoulder, she pinned it to her emerald suit jacket. The catch on the brooch popped open, and she had started to exchange it for another pin when the doorbell rang again.

"Be right there," she called out, hurriedly refastening the brooch. Quickly she slipped into her red pumps and headed for the door. "Coming," she called out as the bell chimed once more, and she hurried down the hall to greet the bodyguard Ryan had sent over. Smiling, she unlocked the door and opened it.

"Dammit, Clea. You didn't even ask who it was."

The good morning she'd been about to utter remained unspoken. Her smile slipped as Ryan stood in the doorway, holding two white paper sacks, and wearing a scowl mean enough to send a prizewinning boxer diving for the corner of the ring.

"What the hell good is a lock and a peephole, if you're just going to open the door and let whoever's on the other side *inside* without even bothering to see who it is first?"

"Good morning to you, too," she said as her eyes raked over him, taking in the black jeans, sweater and boots, and the slightly damp hair. It was a sin against womankind, she decided, that he could look so good this early in the morning with so little effort.

He mumbled something that might have passed for a greeting, then stormed into the apartment. Clea caught the whiff of soap and wind and forest as he moved past her.

"Just where do you think you're going?" she asked when he kept walking, and answered her own question when she followed him into the kitchen. "And what are you doing here, anyway?"

"What does it look like I'm doing?" He set the bags on the table, opened one of them and retrieved two paper cups. He popped off the lids and the scent of fresh, hot coffee filled the small room. He handed one of the cups to her. "I'm bringing you the coffee and doughnuts I promised."

"But I thought..." Clea paused. Nerves jumping, she tried again, "I meant why are *you* here?"

He took a sip of coffee, then sighed. The scowl softened somewhat. "I'm your bodyguard. Remember?"

"Of course, I remember," she told him. How could she possibly forget? "What I want to know is why you're here and not the replacement you sent."

"What replacement?"

"The man sitting across the street," she told him, not up to playing twenty questions with Ryan so early in the morning.

He opened her cabinets, retrieved plates and began filling them with jelly doughnuts. "You mean Jake?"

Clea's mouth watered, reminding her she hadn't even

had coffee yet. She sat down at the table and tried to avoid looking at the calorie-laden feast. "Blond giant with wide shoulders?"

"Yeah. That's Jake," he said, straddling the white birch chair next to hers. He placed two of the doughnuts on the plate in front of her and piled six of the cholesterol nightmares on his own plate. "Jake's not your bodyguard. I am. He just relieved me so I could go clean up, change clothes and pick up our breakfast."

"You do know that this is an absolutely horrible breakfast. Starting your day with all this sugar is terrible for you. Some fresh melon or a bowl of cereal would be much healthier."

Ryan polished off his second doughnut and reached for a third. "Maybe if I were a bird—which I'm not."

No, a bird he wasn't, Clea admitted as she watched him devour the third doughnut and go for a fourth. He was a one-hundred-percent virile and dangerous male.

"I'll admit, bacon and eggs would stick to the ribs a lot better than this, but after watching you eat at the restaurant last night, I figured your refrigerator wouldn't have anything as lethal as bacon and eggs in it. And since I knew I wouldn't have time to shop and buy any, I figured this was the next best thing."

"And I suppose if you had shopped, you'd have expected me to cook breakfast for you," she said, prickling at the little jibe.

"Nah. I noticed last night that fancy stove of yours doesn't look like it gets used much. So, I was prepared to do the cooking since I wasn't sure you knew how."

"Good for you, Sherlock. Because I'm a lousy cook." The cooking had been her sister Desiree's passion, not hers. Hers had been to make a mark in the business world and to someday have her own company.

Ryan paused to take another sip of coffee. "You going to eat that thing or just lust after it."

Clea shot him a cool look, then eyed the tempting treats on her plate with a mixture of love and disdain. Sweets had always been her weakness. She'd have to spend an extra hour on the StairMaster if she hoped to keep the calories from those little suckers off her hips. She gave in to temptation and broke the doughnut in half, scooping a fingerful of raspberry filling into her mouth. She sighed and took a bite.

Ryan smiled, and Clea realized it was the first smile he had given her since walking through the front door. The pleasure she experienced at something so simple as a smile from him surprised her.

"So how'd you sleep last night?"

"Fine," she lied.

"You always walk the floors half the night?"

"I didn't walk the floors half the night." She picked up her gooey doughnut and bit off another piece, her sugar-deprived taste buds savoring the delicious sweet. "I can't imagine why you'd think I did."

"Probably you watching me last night from your window had something to do with it."

Clea flushed. "I just had a little trouble getting to sleep. That's all." When he didn't call her on the lie, she said, "And why were *you* watching my window all night? I told you it wasn't necessary."

The smile disappeared from his face.

For the first time, Clea noted the shadows under his eyes, the lines of strain around his mouth. Tension fisted in her stomach. She put down the doughnut, her appetite suddenly gone. Something was wrong. She could feel it in her bones. "What's wrong? What is it you aren't telling me?"

When he hesitated, Clea pressed. "Whatever it is, I want to know. I have a right."

His eyes zoomed in on her face and before he said a word, Clea knew she wasn't going to like it. "He was here last night," Ryan said softly.

She didn't need Ryan to explain who he meant by "he." They both knew who Ryan was talking about: the caller. Fear bubbled inside her. Her fingers started to shake, so she wrapped them around the cup to keep them still. Swallowing, she willed herself not to panic.

"That beep I got last night, it was from my backup. He'd been coming to bring me some things I needed when he saw someone looking inside your window."

"Did he catch him? Did he see who it was?"

Ryan shook his head. "When the guy spotted my man, he ran. My fellow went after him, but the creep got away. That's when he beeped me. It was too dark to see his face or to be able to identify him. I'm sorry, Clea."

Unable to sit still, she stood. "But you don't know for sure it was the man who's been calling me. I mean you have no way of knowing. Maybe your operative was wrong," she said, grasping at any excuse. She didn't want to believe that he might have been right outside her window, watching her. She didn't want to believe that he might have been watching her at other times, and that she hadn't known. "It could have been some kid playing a prank."

"It wasn't a kid, Clea, and it wasn't a prank. It was him."

"You don't know that! You're just guessing." She twisted the ring on her finger. "You said yourself he probably wouldn't come here."

Ryan sprang to his feet. He reached for her hands, caught her fingers with his own. He held her tight. "I said what I knew you wanted to hear because I wanted to wipe that look of terror out of your eyes. But I was wrong. I shouldn't have lied to you. I won't lie to you ever again."

Panic gripped her like a vise. "He's not going to stop until he gets me, is he?" She hated the fear in her voice. Worse, she hated the despair. But she didn't seem able to stop herself or the words from tumbling out. "And when he does finally get me, he's going to do all those things he threatened to do in the letters...."

"No!" Ryan's hands skated up her arms. He gripped her shoulders. "He isn't going to get you," he told her, his voice hard, his eyes even harder. "Do you hear me, Clea? I'm not going to let him get you."

Then he was pulling her close, pressing her head to his shoulder. "I swear I won't let him hurt you," he murmured, his voice softening along with his touch. "I swear it."

For a moment, the briefest of moments, she clung to him. She, who had sworn never to be weak again, never to depend on a man again and risk being slapped down. She allowed herself to lean on Ryan. To take strength from the feel of his strong arms around her. To take comfort in the soothing stroke of his fingers up and down her spine. To take courage and hope in the soft words of assurance he was whispering against her neck.

Then suddenly something shifted inside her. She became aware of Ryan's heart throbbing frantically beneath her fingers. Of the rock-solid muscles tensing beneath his sweater. Of the heat and heaviness of his arousal nudging against her belly.

The temperature in her kitchen seemed to jump twenty degrees. Her pulse started to race like a car in the final lap of the Indy 500. Her blood began to spin with a sweet, wild ache. She looked up at him, into those incredible blue eyes. Big mistake, she realized as new, lush sensations began to swirl around inside her. Yet it seemed the most natural thing in the world for her to tip her head back. She wanted to ask him to hold her, but couldn't seem to manage the words. Instead, she touched his cheek, then whispered his name. "Ryan."

He swooped down on her lips. He tasted like jelly doughnuts and hot, sweetened coffee with milk. But there was nothing sweet or tame about the way his hands tangled in her hair, or in the way he hauled her body up against his.

Desire slammed through her, nearly knocked her out of her high heels. The woman who prided herself on planning her life and playing in calm, safe waters, had just jumped into a deep river shooting fast toward a waterfall. After his kiss last night, she should have remembered how deep and dangerous and fast those waters could be. But she was having trouble just treading water, let alone remembering to swim the opposite way. How *could* she when every instinct told her to hang on to him?

He released her mouth, and she dragged air into her lungs, only to gasp when his tongue washed over her ear, her neck. His hands were as busy as his mouth. They caressed her face, streaked down her ribs to cup her bottom. Clea moaned as he lifted her, pressed her against him.

Then his mouth was on hers again, sending waves of pleasure and need lapping through her. Even through her skirt, she could feel his arousal, hard and heavy as he rocked against her. His tongue swept inside her mouth and tasted her, mated with hers again while his fingers—those oh-so-clever fingers of his—brushed away her scarf and worked at the buttons of her jacket. He lifted his head and looked at her. The dark, burning need in those deep blue eyes thrilled her, excited her, scared her silly. Her blood started to spin again, and Clea felt herself sliding, closer, closer, dangerously close to the edge of that waterfall. Her eyes drifted shut as Ryan released the last button, only the ivory silk camisole separating her from his touch. Anticipation danced along her nerve endings, and she held her breath as he parted the folds of her jacket.

Then Clea yelped. Her eyes popped open and she jerked back, bumping against the table and sending one of the plates crashing to the floor.

Ryan jumped as though he'd been shot. "Are you all

right? Did I hurt you?" he asked, his voice hoarse, his breathing thready. There was desire and panic in his eyes.

"Yes...No," she said, flustered, finding breathing an effort herself when her body and senses were still singing from the heat of his kisses and touch. She clutched at her shoulder, rubbed at the sharp stinging that lingered. "It's the pin on my scarf. It must have come open and stuck me in the shoulder," she explained, fumbling with the catch.

Ryan brushed her hands away and worked to secure the pin's clasp with fingers that seemed even less steady than hers. Finally, he yanked her jacket closed. Still holding on to the jacket, he rested his forehead against hers, and let out a long breath. "Your kisses pack quite a punch, Duchess."

Right now, she felt as though she was the one who had been punched. She'd all but thrown herself at him. Were it not for that grace-saving stick of her pin, she had little doubt that she would not only not have stopped him from making love to her, but might very well have demanded he do so. Never, not even all those years ago with Eric, had she ever so completely lost control.

Ryan lifted his head and looked into her eyes. He gave her a wry smile. "After that kiss, how am I supposed to keep my hands off you long enough to wrap up this case?"

Clea could feel her skin flush, and she marveled that she had completely forgotten about Ryan's reason for being there. The reminder was as sobering as a glass of ice water thrown in her face. Stepping back, she averted her gaze and refastened the buttons on her jacket. "I'd suggest you try."

He sighed. "I'll do my best, but I have to tell you it won't be easy."

"For the money I'm paying you, it shouldn't matter whether it's easy or not."

He gave her a mock salute at the comeback. "I'll try to keep that thought in mind whenever I find myself considering ripping off your clothes and making love to you."

Which was something they both knew had come very close to happening. "You do that," she said, with a calm that belied the turmoil inside her.

"Well, at least there's one thing that's definitely going to be a piece of cake for both of us," he told her, one of his slow, devilish smiles spreading across his lips.

Clea's senses went on alert. She eyed him warily. "Which is what?"

"Coming up with a convincing cover story for me."

"A cover story?"

"To explain to your friends and co-workers why the two of us are together constantly."

She hadn't thought about that, Clea realized. She had been so caught up in her own reactions to Ryan that she hadn't even considered the full impact having him as her bodyguard would have on her everyday life. Of course, she would need an explanation for his presence. At the least, the people she worked with would require one. Short of telling her co-workers the truth—that a madman was stalking her and that she was afraid—she didn't have a clue what to say. She didn't want to admit just how unnerved and afraid she had been, nor did she want to risk any speculation or fear sprouting up among her staff and especially among her clients.

She should tell Ryan to forget it, that the deal was off. She didn't need or want a bodyguard. She should tell him, Clea repeated to herself. And she would have told him, were it not for the fact that she was even more frightened now that someone had been spotted outside her apartment last night. Frightened enough to wish her sisters were with her. Too frightened to be alone.

Her sisters weren't an option. Ryan was.

And it was fear that made her say, "I suppose you've come up with some sort of story."

"Sure have," he informed her.

Feeling like a rabbit faced with a hungry snake, she asked, "Which is?"

"The obvious. That I'm your lover."

Five

"**W**hat!"

She was looking at him as though he'd lost his mind. And maybe he had, Ryan admitted. How else could he explain that what had started out as a simple gesture of comfort had somehow spiraled into a fire-hot storm of passion? And why, after a glimpse of what heaven it would be to make love to Clea, was he backing off and purposefully pointing out to them both that he had a job to do?

Crazy or not, the flesh-and-blood threat that had stood outside her window last night was every bit as real as the ache in his lower body. It had also been a wake-up call, reminding him of his responsibilities. He needed to remain focused—just as Michael had pointed out. No way should that sicko have gotten past him last night, and the guy wouldn't have if Ryan hadn't been so caught up in Clea. He couldn't afford to let that happen again, Ryan told himself. Just as he couldn't afford to let these strange, new feelings for her growing inside him get in the way of his doing his job. "I think the easiest explanation and the one people will be most likely to believe is that the two of us are lovers."

"No," she said firmly.

There was that word again, Ryan noted with a frown. He was beginning to think it was her favorite word. She certainly used it often enough with him.

"Absolutely not. It's simply out of the question."

"Better get used to the idea because it's the only cover I've been able to come up with that'll explain my being with you around the clock." And after her visitor last night, Ryan intended to stick to her like glue—whether she liked it or not.

"But it's an absurd idea."

"Why?"

"Why?" she repeated, her fingers nervously twisting the button on her jacket. "Because no one's going to believe the two of us are lovers."

"Why not?"

"Because you're…" She shoved her hands down to her sides and looked him straight in the eye. "Because you're not even my type."

The jibe smarted, tempted him to prove her words a lie. Instead, he jammed his hands into his pockets. "It would give me a great deal of pleasure to prove just what a crock that is, but we don't have the time. As soon as we clean up this mess, we need to go. And unless you have a better idea for a cover story, we stick to mine." Not bothering to wait for her agreement, and before he could change his mind about that kiss, he turned away. He stooped down and began picking up the larger shards of glass and dumping them into the waste can.

Silence hung heavily between them for long seconds. Then he heard her heels clicking across the tile and a closet door opening. "You could always say you're a member of the janitorial crew," she offered, handing him the broom.

"Cute." He swept the smaller pieces of glass into a pile and swished them onto the dustpan she held. After dispensing with the mess, he washed his hands at the sink. "Any other ideas?" When she remained silent he said, "Then we go with the lovers' angle."

"No!" Temper flashed in her green eyes. "You're the professional. *You* come up with another idea," she told him, frustration chasing across that gorgeous face of hers.

Ryan wanted to take her in his arms and taste that pouty mouth of hers again. Instead he grabbed the towel and dried his hands. "I already came up with half a dozen last night and ditched them all. Posing as lovers is the only thing that works."

"Oh, you'd like that, wouldn't you?" she said, anger coloring her cheeks.

Ryan couldn't help himself. He grinned. "Can't say that I'd mind."

"Well, I do," she tossed back. "I don't want people to think we're lovers."

"What do you suggest we tell them?"

"I don't know." She yanked a chunk of black hair behind her ear. "Say that you're my brother...or my cousin...or a new travel agent."

Ryan tossed the towel on the counter. Walking over to where she was pacing, he captured her never-still fingers and forced her to stop moving. "Start using that brilliant mind of yours," he said, holding on to her hands when she tried to tug free. "Think! Everyone at the agency knows I'm related to the Donatellis, there's no way I could pull off saying I was your brother or your cousin. And just as many people know I moved here to join my brothers in their security business, so my coming to work at Destinations as a travel agent just won't wash. It also won't provide a reason for my being with you outside of the office."

"But I don't want people thinking we're lovers."

Beautiful *and* old-fashioned, Ryan thought, realizing he liked the combination. "Then tell them we're engaged."

"Engaged!"

"Sure. Everyone who was at that secretary's wedding heard me propose to you. And there's all that superstition stuff. You know, you catching the bouquet, me catching the garter. They'll eat it up. We'll tell people that what started out as a joke turned serious. We've had a whirlwind courtship over the past month and fell in love. I proposed again and this time you accepted."

"That's an even worse idea than the two of us posing as lovers."

"Thanks a lot," Ryan said, taking another hit to his ego. "Believe it or not, there are some women who wouldn't think being engaged to me was such a lousy proposition."

Clea pulled her hands free. "Then I suggest you get one of those women to pretend to be your fiancée instead of me."

His patience slipping, Ryan caught her before she could turn away. "You finished taking pot shots at me? Because if you are, then it's time to wake up, Duchess," he said, his voice harsh. "You're in real trouble here. You need me—"

"I don't need you. I don't need *any* man."

Alarms went off in his head at her heated reply, and Ryan promised himself he would get to the bottom of that one—later. "That's where you're wrong. You *do* need me." When she tried to shrug off his hands, he tightened his grip on her shoulders. "You need me to find the guy who grabbed you at the theater, the one who watched you through your window last night."

She jerked up her chin. Her eyes flashed with defiance, but her skin had gone chalk white. "You're the one who's got it wrong. I don't need you. I'll get someone else to do the job. You're fired."

"Suit yourself." Ryan released her. Irritated with himself for losing his temper, and with her for making him lose it, he walked away. He stared out the window, where the sun was struggling through a patch of clouds to shine on the pitiful strip of grass that was her yard. Her yard. The thing wasn't even big enough for a kid's gym set, he decided, and was surprised by the direction of his thoughts. Everything was perfect and orderly—just like her. Maybe he wasn't her type, but she wasn't his either. So, why in the devil did the thought of walking out of here and leaving her tear at him so much?

"I can write you a check now if you'd like."

Ryan turned around, and damned if his heart didn't kick at the lost look on her face. "Don't worry about it. I'll mail you the bill." Maybe it was for the best, he told himself. He *was* too close to the situation. Too close to her. He had been half joking, half serious when he had told her he wanted to marry her. Desire was no stranger to him. But this new mix of desire and emotion was. And it was screwing with his head. *She* was screwing with his head. He would give them both some space. Let someone else take on the job of protecting her. In the meantime, he'd keep his own watch until the creep harassing her was caught. "I'll post a man outside your apartment and office until you find a replacement."

"Thank you, but that won't be necessary."

Her easy dismissal stung, more than he'd thought it would. "Whatever you say." Without giving her a backward glance, he stormed out of the kitchen and yanked open the door.

The telephone rang and he heard her soft hello.

He paused, telling himself to get out now, fast, while he still could. But he didn't go. He waited.

"Stop it! Do you hear me, stop it! Please, just leave me alone!"

Clea's sobs ripped through him like a knife. Kicking the door shut again, Ryan swore and raced back to the kitchen.

She sat at the table, her hands covering her face, weeping. Great wrenching sobs. The sound slammed into his gut like a bare-knuckled fist, and before he had time to realize just how tangled up in her he was getting, he was kneeling beside her. "It's all right," he whispered as he stroked her hair.

Her head shot up, and she stared up at him out of tear-filled eyes. "I thought you'd gone."

"Changed my mind. Decided I'd rather deal with your sharp tongue than risk getting Aunt Maggie's dander up by walking out on the job. Give it up, Duchess. You're stuck with me."

She went into his arms. "It was him. It was *him!* He wanted to know why I screamed last night. He said that he...that he...."

Something twisted inside him as Clea clung to him and cried. "Shh. Don't think about it. Put it out of your mind for now."

"I'm scared, Ryan. I'm so scared."

"I know, baby. I know. But it's going to be all right. He's not going to get you. I promise." And he intended to keep that promise, Ryan told himself as anger burned inside him. Even if he had to fight Clea to do it, he would keep her safe.

He continued to murmur soothing words for the next few minutes. Finally, when the storm seemed to be over, she lifted her head. "You all right now?" he asked gently.

"Yes." She dropped her arms from around his neck, and he helped her to her feet.

"Thank you," she said, taking a step back. She smoothed her hands down the line of her skirt. "I must look a mess."

Ryan tipped his head as though considering. "Yeah. A real hag."

"Gee, thanks a lot," she said with a laugh.

"Any time. You up to going into the office, or do you want me to call and tell them you won't be in today?"

"No. I'm all right," she said, swiping the last of the tears from her face. "I just need a few minutes to freshen up."

Despite the brave front, there was fear in her eyes and it ate at him like acid. "Take your time. While you're making yourself beautiful again, I'm going to see about getting a tap put on your phone line."

He started to turn away, afraid that if he didn't, he would do something stupid. Like give in to the urge to haul her back into his arms and do whatever he needed to do to erase the fear from her face.

"Ryan."

He paused, at the sound of his name glanced back toward her. "Yeah?"

"I still think it's a bad idea, and I doubt that anyone will be fooled by it, but we'll go ahead with the cover story you came up with."

"Which one?"

"Laugh if you want to, but, I'd prefer we tell people that we're engaged," she said, and then brushed past him and out of the room, leaving him with his mouth hanging open.

She couldn't have been more wrong about how people would react to the story. Not only did no one have any trouble believing she and Ryan were engaged, but they didn't even seem surprised. In the past week even Maggie, who'd been told the truth at the outset, seemed to have forgotten the engagement was a sham. Not that Clea blamed Maggie. Sometimes when Ryan looked at her, put his arm around her, or brushed his mouth against hers in his role as her fiancé, she found herself almost believing the lie, too. Worse, a part of her almost wished it were true.

Clea leaned back in her chair and sighed. And if she had a lick of sense, she would make darn sure she didn't let herself get caught up in her own fabrication. And that's what it was: a fabrication. Oh, she didn't doubt that Ryan found her physically desirable, as she did him. But she had never gone in for casual sex. Sex for her was intricately tangled up with love, and the longing for commitment. And as far as she could tell, none of the Fitzpatrick brothers was interested in the long haul. Not that she blamed them, when women seemed to swarm around them like bees to honey.

But to be fair, Ryan hadn't seemed to be interested in anyone but her. And the idea appealed to her. *What would it be like to be really loved by Ryan?* She smiled. Wonderful, exciting, splendiferous.

Impossible, a voice inside her whispered. The smile slipped from her lips. It was true. Loving Ryan Fitzpatrick, him loving her, would be a colossal mistake—for both of them.

"Clea, I just heard the news," her assistant Gayle exclaimed as she burst into Clea's office. "I can't believe it."

"And just what is it you can't believe, Mrs. Granger?"

The younger woman smiled at the use of her new last name. Even after almost two months, she still had that radiant glow of a new bride. "About your engagement. I had no idea you were seeing Ryan."

"We wanted to keep our relationship low-key," she explained, shifting in her seat. The lies made her uncomfortable, even if they were told for a good reason. She could only hope that when it was all over, everyone would forgive her for the deception.

"Well, you certainly did that."

"How was the cruise? Worth using in our Honeymooners' Special?" Clea asked, eager to change the subject.

"It was fantastic," Gayle said, perching herself on the edge of Clea's desk. "But we'll get back to that later. Right now I want to hear everything. When did he propose? How? Do you have a ring yet?"

"No. No ring." Edgy, Clea stood and grabbed a stack of files from her credenza.

"I'm sure you'll get one later. Ryan strikes me as the possessive type. He'd want people to know you belonged to him."

"We might just use wedding bands," she offered, hating herself for another lie.

"It's so romantic. Like a fairy tale," Gayle said, her eyes as starry as her voice.

"I wouldn't go that far," Clea replied as she deposited the files on her desk.

"Why not? It's true. I mean, think about it. The two of you were at Larry's and my wedding. You caught my bouquet, and Ryan caught the garter. Everyone knows the woman who catches the bridal bouquet is the next to marry. Same thing for the guy who catches the garter. And now the two of you are engaged to marry each other. Why, except for Larry's sudden proposal to me, I don't think I've ever heard of anything more romantic."

Perhaps it would be romantic if it were real, Clea admitted. But the engagement was a sham. She and Ryan weren't a couple. And they certainly weren't in love. The problem was, spending so much time with him, she had gotten to know him better and was beginning to like him too much. Which was something she couldn't afford to let happen because Ryan didn't fit in her plans. Even if she wanted to change that fact, she couldn't.

"He's such a hunk, Clea. And so nice."

"Yes, he is." It was true. Clea glanced across the office to where Ryan was charming the socks off the receptionist and several of the agents. She couldn't help but notice that even in his customary jeans, sweater and boots, he was one of the most gorgeous men she had ever seen. And that mouth. Too bad he couldn't bottle his Irish blarney and sexy grin, he'd make a mint, she thought.

The receptionist's toddler, who had popped in with her

grandmother for a visit, rushed into Ryan's outstretched arms. Clea watched as he lifted her toward the ceiling to retrieve her balloon. Another conquest, she thought. No surprise there. With his movie-star good looks and rakish charm, a female would have to be dead not to fall for him. That was the problem, Clea admitted silently as a sweet yearning unfurled inside her. She was very much afraid she was falling under his spell, too.

The little girl hugged him and planted a kiss on his cheek. Clea's throat tightened. *He's going to make a good father,* she thought, and felt a pang of envy for the woman whose child he would father.

"I heard his business has been kind of slow."

"Yes, but he's expecting it to pick up soon."

"I'm sure it will. But for now, you're really lucky he can spend so much time with you."

"Well, he's not exactly here to just spend time with me. The Donatellis decided we should beef up security now that we've invested so much money in the new computer equipment."

"Yes, I heard. Good idea." Gayle sighed. "I guess I'm just wishing Larry and I could spend more time together."

Something in the younger woman's voice snagged Clea's attention. "Gayle, is everything okay with you two?"

She shrugged. "Nothing that a little more togetherness wouldn't fix."

Guilt pricked at Clea. "I'm sorry. You're still a newlywed and here I am keeping you after hours to work on that corporate retreat program, and then sending you off on a week-long cruise to check it out. I can't believe I've been so selfish."

"Stop apologizing. It's not *my* job that's the problem. It's Larry's."

"But Larry works for himself."

The other woman made a face. "That's just it. He's a freelancer, so he's always off somewhere working on another job. Why just over a week ago, he had a problem getting a system up and running for some big client, and he didn't even get home until well past midnight.''

Clea patted her assistant's hand. ''I'm sorry.'' And she was. Gayle had fallen for Larry Grayden like a ton of bricks the first day he'd walked through the doors of Destinations to present her with a proposal on a new computer system for the firm. By the time the equipment was installed and the kinks worked out, he'd become a familiar fixture at the office and had stolen her assistant's heart. A pleasant, quiet man, his proposal and swift marriage to Gayle had come as a surprise. It saddened Clea to think the couple were having problems. ''Anything I can do? How about a few days off? You could take a long weekend and have Larry go with you to check out one of the resorts on the West Coast that I'm thinking about using for the corporate retreat package.''

''Do you mean it?''

''Absolutely. Why don't you talk it over with Larry tonight, and let me know.'' Since the couple couldn't afford much, it was the least Clea could do. She would run it by Maggie and James when they returned from New York, and if they had a problem, she would pay for the cost of the trip herself.

''Oh, Clea.'' Gayle hugged her, nearly putting Clea's eye out with her chunky earring. ''You're the most wonderful boss. I adore you.''

''Hey, that's supposed to be my line.''

Clea glanced up and discovered Ryan leaning in her office doorway, his arms folded, a smile flirting along his lips. And just as it did every time he was within ten feet of her, her pulse began to race.

Laughing, Gayle straightened and turned to face Ryan. ''It had better be more than a line,'' she told him. ''Your fiancée is one special lady.''

''I know it. It's one of the reason's I want to marry her,''

Ryan said, his eyes serious, his voice sober with none of the teasing she had come to expect from him.

And darned if her foolish heart didn't feel as though it were going to burst in her chest. The way he was looking at her made her almost believe he'd meant what he said.

Gayle sniffed. "From the way you're looking at her, I don't have to ask what the other reasons are."

"And just how am I looking at her?" Ryan asked, a twinge of Irish sneaking its way into his voice.

"Like you'd like to gobble her up whole."

Clea flushed while Ryan's gaze skimmed over her as though he'd like to do just that. Her body tingled all over. Her breath caught in her throat as awareness buzzed between them.

"Nothing wrong with your powers of observation," Ryan returned.

Gayle laughed. "A person would have to be blind not to notice. And I'm not blind."

Neither was anyone else she worked with, Clea mused, mortified by the thought of her co-workers being attuned to the sexual chemistry that sizzled between her and Ryan.

"But I'm warning you. You'd better make my boss happy," she informed him with a wag of her finger. "Because if you don't, I swear, you'll have to answer to me. Understand?"

"You kidding? You've got me shaking in my boots," he said, and ruined it by winking. "Don't worry, I'll make Clea happy—or die trying."

And he was the kind of man who would make a woman deliriously happy, Clea thought, both in and out of bed. But some other woman, she reminded herself. Not her.

"What do you say, darling? Think your dragon-slaying assistant here would mind if I stole you away for the rest of the afternoon?"

"No problem," Gayle said.

"I can't go."

Ryan chuckled, his gaze bobbing between her and Gayle. "Which is it?"

"I have a lot of work to do this afternoon," Clea replied. The last thing she needed was to spend more time alone with Ryan.

"Nothing that I can't handle or that can't wait until tomorrow," Gayle informed her. "I checked your calendar on my way in from the airport. You don't have any appointments until tomorrow morning."

Ryan came around the desk and brushed his mouth, soft as a whisper, against hers. "What do you say? Play hooky with me? It's for a good cause."

"What's the good cause?" she asked, her voice husky, betraying his effect on her.

"Picking out your engagement ring."

Clea nearly choked as the air was sucked out of her lungs. Gayle let loose with a very unbusinesslike squeal that had heads in the outer office lifting and turning to stare at them. Her legs shaky, Clea gripped the edge of her desk. "Ryan, I really think we need to discuss this—in private."

"Whatever you say, darling," he said, capturing her fingers in one hand and retrieving her purse from her desk drawer with the other. He handed her the bag and ushered her toward the door. "But we'll need to talk on the way. We have an appointment at the jewelers."

Fifteen minutes later, Ryan practically shoved her through the doors of the small, elegant Chicago jewelry store. "This is ridiculous," Clea argued, coming to a halt. "I don't need an engagement ring!"

Everything and everyone seemed to come to a complete stop at her outburst. Clea closed her eyes a moment, mortified by the scene she was creating. *Please, I'll give up my IRAs and surrender my blue-chip stocks, just let a hole materialize and swallow me up.* But the god who passed out those holes evidently didn't hear her, because when she opened her eyes, she was still there—right next to Ryan.

"Of course you need an engagement ring," Ryan said cheerily as he started to tug her along.

"Take my advice, deary," an elderly woman, with diamond studs in her ears the size of walnuts, told Clea in a stage whisper that could be heard clear across the store. "Let him buy you the ring."

"See? Even she agrees you need an engagement ring." Ryan winked at the older woman and said, "My fiancée's a little nervous about the wedding—bridal jitters."

"First wedding?"

"Yes," Ryan told her. "For both of us."

"I understand. I remember my first wedding night," she said with a sigh.

Color raced up Clea's cheeks. *Forget the hole. Just give me a big rock. I'll crawl under it myself.*

"Given the looks of this one, my guess is you'll be more than satisfied," the older woman said, eyeing Ryan up and down like a boy-hungry sixteen-year-old.

"Why, thank you, ma'am."

Grabbing Ryan by the arm, Clea curled her nails into the sleeve of his sweater and dug them in. "*Darling,* let's not keep the jeweler waiting," she said sweetly and practically dragged him away from Diamond Lil. "You're a dead man, Fitzpatrick," Clea muttered as they waltzed deeper into the store.

"Ryan! Ryan, over here."

Clea's heart lurched at the sight of the tall, gorgeous brunette in a security uniform standing next to a display case and waving to Ryan.

Ryan's eyes lit up. "Molly!" Abandoning Clea, he rushed over to the brunette, caught her up in his arms and spun her around. She laughed, that confident, sexy, feminine laugh most women could never hope to imitate. When Ryan set her on her feet again, he gave her a loud, smacking kiss. "You look wonderful."

Talk about understatements, Clea thought morosely, feeling like last year's prom dress as she stared at the striking brunette in Ryan's arms. Together they were stunning, she admitted, noting the other woman's long, lithe figure and dark-as-night hair fitted next to Ryan's tall, sturdy frame. And the picture of them together gave Clea a sinking feeling in the pit of her stomach.

"Thanks," Molly said, a pretty blush climbing up her model-perfect cheekbones. "You don't look so bad yourself."

"So, what on earth are you doing here?"

"Working security detail for the store."

"Given up on being a cop?" Ryan asked.

She snickered. "Do elephants fly? I'm just waiting to hear if I've been accepted by the guys at State for the next class."

Ryan whistled. "State, huh? I'm impressed."

"You will be—when I'm accepted," she told him, with a bravado that didn't quite match the nervousness in her eyes.

"You'll be accepted," Ryan assured her.

"I sure hope you're right."

"So, where's your dad? I have an appointment with him."

"I heard," Molly said with a smile. "He called to say he's running a little late from an appointment across town. He'll be here shortly. In the meantime," she said, looking past Ryan to Clea. "Why don't you introduce me to the brave woman who's agreed to marry you?"

"You mean the lucky woman," Ryan corrected.

Molly gave a most unladylike snort. "Brave. Definitely brave," she repeated and extended her hand to Clea. "Hi, I'm Molly Fitzpatrick."

Clea froze in the process of shaking Molly's hand. She'd been prepared to meet a former girlfriend, possibly a lover, but the name had thrown her. Was she his wife? An icy chill crawled up her spine at the thought. And for the space of a heartbeat, Clea thought she was going to be ill, before common sense reared its head. Ryan would hardly announce their engagement if he were already married. "Did you say your name was Fitzpatrick?"

"Yes. Ryan and I are first cousins."

Relief washed over her like a tidal wave racing to shore. "I'm Clea Mason."

"Yes, I know," she said with a smile. "Your name's been buzzing all over the family grapevine."

Clea arched a brow and looked at Ryan. "The family grapevine?"

He rolled his eyes. "The Fitzpatrick gossip machine. It's a family network headed by my mother and of which my nosy little cousin here is a member."

"Ignore him, Clea. Ryan has never fully appreciated what a close-knit family we are."

"You mean a nosy family," he said with affection in his voice.

Molly sniffed and made a face at him. "As I was saying, we're all pretty close and because we are, we sort of keep tabs on one another. You can't imagine how surprised we were when we learned about Ryan's and your engagement."

"I realize it was rather sudden," Clea said, not liking the idea of Ryan's family being drawn into their deception.

"But so exciting. It's the biggest news to hit the family since that scandal with Connor—"

"Molly. Stick to the subject," Ryan said, something fierce in his voice at the mention of his brother.

"Right. Like I was saying, it's the biggest news in ages."

"You make it sound like no one in your family's ever gotten engaged before," Clea told her.

"You mean you don't know?"

Clea could feel a headache coming on, sure she wasn't

going to like the answer to her next question. "Know what?"

"That Ryan and his brothers are the only male offspring in the Fitzpatrick family. My pop and the rest of his brothers all produced girls—except for Uncle Keagan, Ryan's dad. That means Ryan and his brothers are the ones responsible for carrying on the Fitzpatrick name." Molly made a face and continued, "That's something that doesn't seem really fair to me since it's the woman who actually does all the hard work, but that's another story. Anyway, my dear cousin here is the first of the Fitzpatrick brothers to fall."

"Fall?" Clea repeated, growing more uncomfortable by the second at the conversation.

"You know, the big *C* word—commitment. Marriage. We were beginning to think none of them would ever get married." Molly placed an arm around Clea's shoulders as though they were long-lost buddies. "Shoot, my poor aunt Isabel—Ryan's mom—she's been saying novenas for years, praying for one of her boys to marry. She said she was beginning to lose hope. And then, out of the blue, you come along. You, my dear cousin-to-be, are the answer to my aunt's prayers."

"Actually, I wouldn't go quite that far. I mean Ryan and I, that is, we are—"

"What Clea's trying to say, Cuz, is to hang on to the rice. Geez. We just got engaged. Clea doesn't have her ring yet, and we haven't even discussed a wedding date."

"Ryan's right," Clea added.

Molly simply smiled. Her dark eyes gleamed with the same hint of mischief Clea had seen often enough in all four Fitzpatrick brothers to make her worry. "Well, *Cuz*," she said, stressing the family endearment. "If I were you, I wouldn't count on a long engagement. Last I heard, your mom's already knitting baby booties."

Six

"**A** perfect fit," Morgan Fitzpatrick declared as Ryan slipped the engagement ring onto Clea's finger.

Ryan stared down at the small, slender hand where the gold and diamond heirloom ring—worn by Fitzpatrick brides for four generations—gleamed under the store lights. "It's as though the ring were made for you," he told Clea, feeling a strange warmth and glow in his chest. He hadn't planned to give her a ring as part of the cover story they had concocted, hadn't even considered it—until his mother had got wind of the engagement. After tearing a strip off him for not telling her he was getting married, she'd insisted he have the ring cleaned and polished, and present it to his future bride. He had given in, knowing he'd have to deal with the consequences later when the truth came out, but determined nonetheless to keep the lid on the situation until he ferreted out Clea's stalker. But now, seeing the ring on Clea's hand, he felt a rush of pride and, surprisingly, an unexpected longing for the engagement to be real.

"Ryan, we really need to be going. I have some work to do tonight."

His gaze jumped from the ring to Clea's face. The panic in those wide green eyes of hers hit him like a sucker punch to the jaw. Evidently, *he* was the only one with those crazy romantic notions.

"Ryan?"

"She's right, Uncle Morgan. We really do need to be going." Forcing a smile he didn't feel, he shook his uncle's hand. "Thanks again for the rush job on the ring."

"My pleasure. The family's waited a long time for one of you boys to take a wife. We were all beginning to worry that the Fitzpatrick name would die out. But now," he said, bestowing another smile on Clea, his salt-and-pepper mustache twitching above his lips, "the family can rest easy. You've chosen well, Ryan."

"I think so, too," Ryan said, feeling guilty over the hopes that were raised by the announcement of his engagement. He shifted uncomfortably. "We really do need to go. Be sure to give Aunt Liz a hug for me."

"Will do, my boy." He slapped Ryan on the back and enveloped Clea in a bear hug. "Welcome to the family, Clea."

"Thank you, Mr. Fitzpatrick," she said, her discomfort obvious from the stiffness of her body.

"Uncle Morgan," he corrected as he released her. "We're family now."

"Uncle Morgan," she repeated, darting a glance at Ryan that said "get me out of here."

After thanking his uncle again, Ryan gave a mock salute to his cousin at the other side of the store and, taking Clea's hand, turned to leave.

"Goodbye," Uncle Morgan said again. "Aunt Elizabeth and I will look forward to seeing you at the engagement party."

Clea paused mid-step and spun around. "The engagement party?"

"Yes," his uncle informed her, the smile lines around his eyes deepening like ruts in a dirt road. "The one Isabel's planning for the two of you. Didn't she tell you?"

"Yeah, she did. We'll see you there," Ryan told him, and hustled Clea toward the exit. He'd hoped to break that bit of news to her later—after he'd gotten her past the shock of the engagement ring and the anxiety that had been mounting in her ever since they'd left the office. Now, thanks to his uncle, he no longer had the option of picking the time and place.

"What engagement party is he talking about?" she demanded as Ryan led her through the store and out of his uncle's earshot.

"It's my mother's idea. She wants the family to meet you." Her hand stiffened in his, and he let out a sigh. "I was going to tell you later, but it happened sort of fast, and I never got the chance. I tried to talk her out of it, but my mother wouldn't take no for an answer. The best I could do was get her to hold off for a couple of weeks. She'd already booked the caterers before she even called me."

Clea stopped and stared at him as though he had suddenly spouted two heads. "Are you out of your mind?"

"I'm beginning to wonder," he said wearily, already sensing the battle to come. He urged her outside the store and started walking toward his car. Might as well spit out the rest of the news. "We're also having dinner with my parents this weekend."

Clea stopped again and this time there was no mistaking the fact that she saw see him as some kind of monster. Dark clouds stretched over the sky, blocking out the fading sunlight like a shade drawn over a window and framing Clea in its muted shades of smoke. She looked incredibly fragile and beautiful. "Please," she whispered. "Tell me you're joking. That everything that's happened today is just a bad dream.''

"Afraid not.''

For a moment, he thought she was going to cry, and felt a stab of guilt for being the cause. Wind whistled down the street, sending her dark locks dancing across her mouth. She shoved the hair away from her face. "You have to cancel it,'' she told him, her voice anxious.

He wanted to touch her, to soothe away those nerves jumping inside her and making her eyes seem even larger in her pale face. But if he touched her, he was afraid he would lose another piece of himself to her. The thought unsettled him. He had never lost himself in a woman before and didn't like the fact that it made him feel vulnerable. "I can't.''

"You *have* to,'' she insisted, her voice just short of frantic. "I can't go. I *won't* go. Not to the engagement party or to dinner with your parents. It's bad enough I've got to wear this ring and pretend we're engaged,'' she said, eyeing the ring as though it were a poisonous snake. "I refuse to turn this...this mockery into an even bigger hoax on your family.''

"Get a grip,'' Ryan told her, taken aback by her outburst. She was like a high-strung filly at the starting gate of the track. He caught her hand, held it in his until she seemed to settle somewhat. Then something shifted. Suddenly, the awareness was spinning between them again. Ryan could see it in her eyes, feel it in the new tension in her body. He rubbed his thumb across the finger wearing his ring. "It doesn't have to be a hoax, Clea,'' he told her, the words spilling out of him without warning, air backing up in his lungs.

"But it *is* a hoax.''

"Not if we make the engagement real.''

Clea sucked in a breath. Her eyes widened in shock, and

she tugged her hand free. She looked at him as though he had slapped her. "That would be even worse."

Then she took off down the street in a walk that was just short of a run. Stunned, for several moments Ryan stood in the middle of the sidewalk and watched her. She had been terrified. There was no other word to describe the out-and-out panic he had seen chase across her features.

Pain ripped through him like a knife, catching him off guard. He had wanted a woman before, had been turned down once or twice, and had suffered little more than a dent to his ego. But this time it was different. Maybe because *she* was different. Oh, he wanted her, all right, he admitted. No denying that fact. His hormones had been at Mach speed since the first time he'd seen her. And hundreds of cold showers since then hadn't slowed them down. Hell, a thousand cold showers wouldn't have done any good because he wanted Clea in a way he'd never wanted another woman. Wanted her in a way he feared he'd never want another woman again.

But it was more than sex, and he knew it. He cared about her. She had somehow snuck into his heart and become important to him. More important than anyone had ever been before. More important than he wanted her to be. The realization shook him, scared him right down to his toes. When in the devil had these feelings for her ambushed him? And what was he going to do about those feelings when just the idea of being engaged to him sent her running like a fox with a pack of hounds on her tail?

Hurt sliced at him like a whip as he remembered her rejection. And on the heels of that hurt, came anger. Irrational, over-the-top anger. Who did she think she was? Kicking his proposal—fumbled though it was—back in his teeth? Did she think he would just tuck his tail between his legs and scurry away like those fancy-suited nerds with the pretty hands she seemed to prefer? If she did, then she didn't know Ryan Fitzpatrick.

Adrenaline pumping, he took off after the slender figure in lemon silk, beelining down the street. A bus unloaded, and he untangled himself from the rush of passengers, struggling to see that Clea made it safely to the car.

But when she reached the car, instead of waiting for him, she walked right past it. Damn! "Clea," Ryan called out, alarmed. It was getting dark. She was alone, and though there had been no calls since they had announced their engagement, Ryan didn't trust that the crazy who had been after her had given up. Apologizing, he elbowed his way through the bus crowd in time to see Clea cross the street to the next block.

Oh, but he was going to enjoy watching her eat that rejection. And she would eat it, he promised himself as he picked up his pace.

Suddenly she let loose a high-pitched whistle that even he would have been proud to claim and waved at an approaching taxi. He would enjoy it, he amended as he broke into a run, if he didn't wind up ringing her pretty neck first. "Clea, wait!"

The taxi slowed, pulled over to the curb and began easing up alongside of her. Ryan reached her at the same time she opened the taxi's door. He slapped it shut and grabbed her around the waist. "Beat it," he told the driver.

"No!"

When the guy hesitated, he said, "It's all right. She's my fiancée, and we've just had a little lovers' spat. You go ahead. I'll see that she gets home safely."

"That's not true. He's lying. We're not engaged!"

But the taxi was already moving down the street, seeking a new fare. Ryan released her. "That was a pretty stupid thing to do," he lashed out.

Clea made a noise that was part frustration, part rage. She swung around, fire burning in her eyes, and took a swing at him.

Ryan caught the fist determined to clip his jaw. She

aimed for his face with her other fist. He trapped that one, too. For the life of him, he still wasn't sure what had made him propose to this hellcat, or why her refusal had slashed him to ribbons. She kicked him in the shin. Ryan swore. Her temper fed his own.

"You don't want to push me right now, Duchess," he warned her, anger still clawing at him like a beast as he thought of what might have happened had she been able to escape. He remembered the sick ravings in the last letter and his blood chilled. What if the wacko had been waiting for her at home before Ryan could get there to check it out first?

Evidently something in his expression made her reconsider, because she stopped trying to take a poke at him. "You're hurting me," she accused.

Ryan eased his grip. "Let's go. I'll take you home."

She jerked her wrist free as they started to walk. "I don't want or need you to drive me home," she told him, rubbing at her wrist. "I'm taking a taxi."

"Wrong. *I'm* taking you home." He placed a hand at the small of her back and urged her forward. She dug in her heels. Exasperated, Ryan leaned closer and dropped his voice to a low dangerous whisper, "We can do this the easy way or the hard way. Your choice. But make no mistake, I *am* going to take you home. Now what's it going to be? Do you walk to the car, or do I carry you?"

She set her hands on her hips. "You wouldn't dare."

"You're right," he said, and moved as though to walk away from her, only to whip around and grab her. She shrieked as he slung her over his shoulder. "Big mistake, Duchess," he said, smacking her bottom when she started to kick. "I'm one of those fellows who could never pass on a dare."

"You're fired," Clea told him furiously as he ignored her protests and carted her down the street like a sack of potatoes.

After saluting the openmouthed couple who had stopped to watch them, Ryan unlocked the car door and dumped her into the passenger seat. "Buckle up."

"I said, you're fired!"

"I heard you, Duchess. But it's obvious you're not thinking clearly right now so I'm going to pretend I didn't hear you."

Clea bristled. "There's nothing wrong with my thinking processes. They're as sharp and clear as they've always been. And I'm firing you as of right now."

He blocked the door when she started to get out. "If you were thinking straight, we both know you wouldn't do something foolish like take off by yourself," he said, his voice dangerously soft, his expression fierce. "And we know you wouldn't even consider getting into a car with a stranger who could easily turn out to be the guy who's been threatening you."

The statement hit her like a slap. She drew in a sharp breath. "He wasn't a stranger. He was a taxi driver. He had a taxi and a driver's ID."

"Taxis can be stolen. ID's can be faked."

"They were real," she countered. But the truth was that it hadn't crossed her mind to think otherwise. All she'd been thinking about was getting away from him, away from the ache squeezing her heart like a merciless fist when he'd offered to make the engagement real. She'd known he was trouble right from the start—but she'd been scared enough to risk dancing with those deep-down emotions and longings he'd awakened in her.

"You don't know that. The guy has been smart enough to cover his tracks by scrambling the phone lines when he calls so that I can't get an accurate trace on him. He's smart enough to use common, dime-store stationery that's nearly impossible to trace back to him. What makes you think he couldn't pull off something like a fake taxicab and ID? The man seems to know where you go, what you wear, who you're with. What makes you think he didn't know you came with me to the jewelers this afternoon?''

A chill slid down her spine, and she folded her arms across her chest to keep from shuddering. She forced herself to meet Ryan's angry gaze. ''He couldn't know. *I* didn't know I was coming here until the last minute.''

''But everyone else knew.''

''They couldn't have known, I—''

''You can bet my whole family knew. Which meant Uncle James and Aunt Maggie knew. Not to mention your assistant Gayle.''

''Which means the rest of the office knew,'' Clea added, knowing that Gayle's only fault as her assistant was her eagerness to chat. And when she was excited or happy about something, as she was about Ryan's and her engagement, Gayle's enthusiasm would make it impossible for her to keep the news to herself. Everyone in the office, and probably half of the clients who might have phoned in, would know that Clea had gone to get her engagement ring.

''You can bet on it,'' Ryan said smugly. ''And if your pen pal knew we were coming here, he might also have witnessed our little tiff. Supposing he had? Supposing he saw you storm off and leave me, and decided tonight would be a good time to go back to your apartment and wait for you?''

''Stop it!'' It had been four days since the last phone call. She wanted to believe it was over, and resented Ryan for taking away even that small piece of comfort. ''You're just trying to make me believe that whoever's behind the letters and phone calls is someone I know.''

''My gut tells me it is.''

''Then your gut is wrong. It has to be somebody else. No one I know would ever do such a thing.''

''You'd be amazed at what lengths a man will go to to

get a woman he wants. For instance, if I decided you were what I wanted, you can bet nothing on this earth would stop me from making it a reality.''

Something in his voice made her look back at him. No devilish smile curved those lips now. No mischief winked in those blue eyes. Even the anger that had all but vibrated from him moments ago had been replaced by a rock-hard determination. It was there in the set of his jaw, in the glint of steel in his eyes. Clea couldn't shake the feeling that she'd just been issued a warning. The thought sent a nervous shudder of anticipation through her. ''You're just trying to scare me,'' she said through lips that were suddenly desert-dry.

''You're right, I am,'' he said with a ruthlessness that was razor-sharp and every bit as stinging. ''I want you to be scared. So scared that you won't take off again like you did tonight. Scared enough to trust me when I tell you I'll keep you safe.''

''I trust you,'' she admitted. Because she did. Physically, she felt safe knowing he was nearby or just outside her apartment at night. Emotionally it was another story, she conceded as he shut her door and walked around to the driver's side. How could she feel safe when the man churned her up inside? Made her want him, made her want things she knew she could never have? She stared down at the ring on her finger, and that vice in her chest squeezed a notch tighter around her heart.

The door next to her opened and closed. He slid into his seat. After a moment of silence, he turned to her. ''I'm sorry if I was rough on you,'' he said, his voice gentler than it had been moments before.

No, don't do this to me. Don't be nice. Because if he was nice to her, she couldn't be angry with him. And without anger, she didn't stand a chance of resisting him. Ignoring her silent plea, he brushed his thumb along her jaw, and she was hard-pressed not to turn her mouth into his palm. She didn't know where the strength came from, but she forced herself to pull back from his touch.

The warmth disappeared faster than a runaway train. He wrapped his fingers around the steering wheel as though he wished it were her throat. "I don't like the lies any more than you do, Clea. But we don't have any choice. We have to keep up the charade."

"Couldn't we at least tell your family the truth?"

"No," he said firmly. "The fewer people who know the truth, the better. If it's any consolation, I won't be enjoying this sham any more than you will."

In fact, he looked like he'd like nothing better than to wash his hands of her right now. And she didn't blame him, Clea told herself.

"If you need something to focus on, to get you through the horrible ordeal of playing my loving fiancée for the next few days, you might concentrate on the fact that this guy's going to slip up sooner or later. When he does, I'll be there to nab him. And once I do, the two of us won't ever have to see each other again."

The verbal smack hurt, just as did the realization that what he said was true. When this was all over, Ryan would be gone from her life. He'd find a woman who deserved to wear his ring, a woman who deserved his love. That woman wasn't her. Feeling more depressed by the minute, Clea stared out the window at the lights of the city and tried to ignore the empty ache inside her.

For the next twenty minutes silence hung between them as thick as smoke, as heavy and oppressing as the humidity on a summer day down south. He'd apologized to her twice now for carting her like a sack of potatoes down the street and for springing the engagement ring and party on her. She'd accepted the apology both times, and conversation died off. But she sensed an edginess in him as he drummed his fingers on the steering wheel. He punched the car's accelerator when the light changed to green, only to race to the next corner and screech to a halt at the light.

"You planning to sulk much longer?"

His accusation pulled her from her unhappy thoughts.

"I don't sulk," she informed him.

Ryan snorted. "Could have fooled me."

"Then you're a man who's easily fooled," she tossed back, heedless of the storm she sensed brewing in him.

"Don't bet on it," he muttered before taking off again from the light. He switched lanes and sent the car flying forward. Her heart in her throat, for a crazy moment Clea remembered his comments about her driving skills or lack thereof. She had to bite her tongue to keep from snipping at him about his. He was taking on a strong resemblance to a restless tiger she'd once seen at a circus, and she saw no sense in prodding him with a hook.

Evidently, he didn't need any prodding, she decided. As the car's speedometer climbed, so it seemed did Ryan's irritation. "How many more times am I going to have to apologize before you get over this snit you're in? I've already said I was sorry for embarrassing you back there. And I explained how my mother insisted I give you the ring. I couldn't very well refuse her without blowing our cover."

"I said I understood. I just don't agree with you about lying to your family. I don't see why we can't just tell them the truth. It's not like you suspect any of them, right?"

"Until I catch the guy sending those letters and calling you, everyone's a suspect."

Shocked, she stared at him. "Including your own family?"

"I'm not ruling out anybody at this point. My brothers know you, see you socially. So does my uncle James."

"That's absurd, and you know it."

"Why? They're men. You're an attractive woman. Who's to say it's not one of them?"

"I'm saying it. Sean and Michael are like…like brothers to me. And your uncle, well, James is almost a second father to me."

"But Michael and Sean aren't your brothers. And my uncle isn't your father," Ryan pointed out, a scowl darkening his face. "They're men," he told her, pulling the car to a stop in front of her apartment. He shut off the engine and turned toward her. "My brothers are always in and out of the agency. And my uncle works with you, he's privy to your comings and goings."

He was serious, Clea realized. Acid pitched in her stomach at the thought of Sean or Michael or James being responsible for the notes and phone calls. "So are half a dozen other people in the office."

"Which is why every one of them is on my list of suspects."

"Well, you can just scratch their names off that list. We both know your brothers have enough females chasing them. They don't need to resort to sick notes and phone calls."

"And my uncle?"

"In case you've forgotten, your uncle's a married man and very much in love with his wife."

"He's also a man with a wife who happens to be busy a lot lately since she started her new business. I couldn't help but notice how often my uncle calls you—even when you're at home."

"Of course James calls me. Why shouldn't he? I work for him. He has every right to expect me to report to him about the business."

"Is that why he sent roses to your apartment last week? And the lunch invitation he issued yesterday, the one he rescinded when I insisted on coming along. Was the invitation extended because he wanted a private report from you on the state of the business?"

Anger knotted her insides. "I'm not even going to dignify that with an answer." And she also had no intention of divulging the fact that James was worried that Maggie was seeing someone else and had been coming to Clea for marital advice.

"Would you like me to supply you with the answer I've come up with?"

"No."

She started to turn away and he captured her wrist. "I'll give it to you anyway. I think my uncle may very well be your caller."

"I'm not going to listen to this garbage." She jerked her wrist free and quickly unfastened her seat belt, which suddenly felt like a restraining jacket.

"I think my uncle's obsessed with you. That he believes himself to be in love with you."

"You're wrong!" Hands trembling with fury, she finally managed to release the seat belt.

"Am I, Clea? Am I?"

"Yes," she hurled the word back as she fumbled with the lock on the door.

"I don't think so. You see, I know firsthand what it's like to hold you, to kiss you and not be able to get the taste of you off my lips. I know what it's like to close my eyes at night and not be able to sleep for wanting you. Desire that powerful can drive even the strongest of men to do something crazy. And my uncle James isn't a strong man. Ten years ago he had an obsession with the bottle, and he—"

"Stop it. You have no right telling me these things about James."

"I have every right to tell you. It's my job to make sure nothing happens to you. To do that, I need to make sure you know who you can and can't trust."

"And I suppose the only person I can trust is *you*. Is that it?" she demanded, furious with him for casting shadows on the people she cared about. For leaving her no one to turn to but him.

"Pretty close," he told her.

His arrogance caused something inside her to snap. "Well, you lose this one, Fitzpatrick. Because I do trust James. I don't know what happened to him ten years ago, and I don't want to know. I know that he's my friend, and he'd never do what you're accusing him of."

The lock snicked open and she pushed her way out of the car. Slamming the door shut, she hurried toward her apartment, desperate to get away from Ryan, from all his suspicions, from all the feelings he churned up inside her.

"Clea, wait!"

She heard him swear, then a car door smack shut as he came after her. She sprinted the distance to her apartment and up the row of stairs.

"Let me go in first and check the place out," he said from behind her.

"I don't need you to check it out. I can take care of myself. Just take your nasty suspicions and go away." Pushing her hair back from her face, she dug in her purse for her keys. She snagged the metal disk, and with trembling fingers aimed the key at the lock.

"Give me the keys, Clea."

"No," she told him, determined to get inside, to get away from him, to lock him out of her apartment and her heart for good. The key slammed home and she felt a burst of triumph as she shoved the door open.

"Dammit, Clea. I said let me go in first!"

"No," she told him and rushed inside. "I told you, I don't need—"

Her heart stopped. Her blood chilled in her veins as she stared at the envelope propped up against the vase of flowers on the table.

"What is it? Clea, what's wrong?" Ryan asked grimly. He took a step around her, walked over and stared at the

envelope with her name written in that all-too-familiar
scrawl.

Clea heard a wounded animal's wail, and only when the
sound grew louder, more terrified, did she realize it was
coming from her.

Seven

Something tightened inside him as he listened to the sounds coming from her—like those of a frightened, wounded kitten. Ryan caught her face in his hands. "Clea, listen to me. It's all right. Do you hear me? It's all right. I'm here."

She threw herself against him and clung so desperately that he expected her nails to dig right through his shirt to his skin and draw blood. He wrapped his arms around her trembling body and held her close. While he stroked her back, he sized up the situation at a glance. The former cop in him told him they were alone, but he scanned the room and listened for movement from other parts of the apartment anyway. Nothing. Just the letter. Acid rolled in his stomach as he recalled the filth he'd read in the others. He had no doubts this one would contain more of the same.

Long seconds ticked by. She shuddered again and he waited for the whimpers to turn into tears. They didn't. Instead the heart-wrenching sound slowed, then stopped altogether. After a moment he said, "I need to check the apartment. Will you be okay?"

Her head bobbed against his shoulder, and she gave him a muffled "yes."

Gently, Ryan eased her away from him, but she retained the viselike grip she had on him. He tipped up her chin to assess the damage. Her face was ghostly pale, but she hadn't shed a single tear and she appeared to be all right. He hated to leave her for even a second, but knew he had to. "I'll only be a couple of minutes, but I want you to stay put and don't touch anything. Understand?"

She nodded again, and this time released him. Satisfied she would be okay, he drew the gun strapped at the back of his waist, released the safety and started down the hall.

A long five minutes later, he reset the safety, tucked his gun away and returned to the living room and Clea. She sat on the edge of the fancy designer couch, a fragile figure in lemon silk, with her hands resting in her lap, her fingers laced together in a white-knuckled clasp. Under the light of a nearby lamp, her usually creamy complexion had turned the color of chalk. And her eyes, those big liquid green eyes that could freeze a man in his tracks or make him burn with desire, were glassy with tears she refused to let fall.

As though sensing his presence, she glanced up. "Any sign of him?" she asked, her voice a hoarse whisper of fear that she was doing her damnedest to tame.

"No," Ryan replied, noting her shoulders unbend a little. "From the looks of things, I'd say he didn't go beyond this room. I've still got a few more things I want to check out though, and then I'll need to dust for prints."

"Fingerprints," she said her eyes resting on the table where the note still lay. "If you get his prints, then you'll be able to find out who he is and make him stop."

The hope in her voice made his heart ache because he couldn't allow her even that little comfort. "I have to be honest with you, Duchess. I doubt that I'll find any prints. This guy's been very smart up to now. The only slip he's made was grabbing you at the theater, and even that trail was a dead end because you never saw him. I doubt he'd be foolish enough to break in here and not wear gloves."

"You're right, of course."

"I'm sorry," Ryan said, frustrated at feeling so helpless.

"No. You were right to tell me. I need to know the truth. It's just that every time I think about him being here inside my home, touching my things…" She stared past him as though she were looking at ghosts.

"I doubt that he touched anything," he told her, offering what little comfort he could. "More than likely he came in, left the letter on the table and cut out."

"The letter. I guess I should read it."

"You don't need to." Ryan picked up the envelope with his handkerchief and carefully pulled out the note. Acid rolled in his stomach as he read. "It just says the same sort of stuff the others did," he told her and eased the sheet back into the envelope. Except that this one was worse than the other letters. The tone was more twisted, more demanding, more desperate. If he could do nothing else, he would spare her from that.

She shivered and Ryan was beside her in a heartbeat. "What is it?"

"I was just thinking what if you hadn't stopped me, if I had taken that taxi and arrived here earlier by myself—"

"Don't, Clea. Don't do this to yourself," he warned, feeling another kick to his gut when she shuddered again.

"He might have been here waiting for me when I came in."

He couldn't deny it, Ryan realized, furious with himself for not following through on his instincts to have a guard posted on the place around the clock. "Then he'd have had to face both of us. There was no way I'd have let you come back here without me. And I'm not going to leave you alone.''

Her gaze rose to meet his. ''I'm scared, Ryan. Really scared.''

''I know, baby. I know.'' He captured those cold fingers of hers, wrapped them in his hands. ''You're entitled.'' She was more than entitled, he amended silently. Most women in her shoes would have been wailing like a banshee by now after the fright she'd had. But not his Clea. She was made of stronger stuff—only now the starch in her stuffing looked a bit limp.

''He's going to get me, isn't he? It's just a matter of time before he does.''

The resignation and defeat in her voice damn near tore his heart out. ''Listen to me. He is not going to get you. I won't let him get you.''

Gentling his voice, he said, ''I know I've done a lousy job of protecting you so far. I don't blame you for not believing I can keep you safe.''

''I didn't say that. And I'm not blaming you, Ryan.''

Maybe she didn't blame him, but he sure blamed himself. After three weeks, he should have had more than a list of possible suspects, a stack of letters and taped calls that led to dead ends. He should have had the jerk behind bars by now. Was it because he was too close to the case, too involved emotionally? Had he missed some telltale clue, something that would have saved her from going through this torment? Or was it because he didn't want to accept the fact that the culprit might be his uncle?

''I know I was upset about the fake engagement and was kind of rough on you earlier. But despite the things I said, I do know you've done everything you can to help me.''

Only his everything hadn't been good enough. The guy was still out there somewhere, probably planning his next move. Ryan didn't know what that move would be, but judging from today's letter, that next move would be soon.

"I appreciate the vote of confidence, but if you want to hire someone else, I'll understand. In fact, maybe it would be a good idea if you did. I could talk to Michael if you'd like, see if he could free himself up to—"

"Running out on me, Fitzpatrick? After railroading me into hiring you in the first place?"

"No. It's just that I haven't exactly been holding up my end of the bargain."

"As far as I'm concerned, you have. I don't want Michael or anyone else. I want you, Ryan Fitzpatrick. If you can't stop him, then no one can."

But despite the brave little speech, she didn't believe he could stop the man. He could see in her eyes the resignation that the maniac stalking her would eventually succeed. Her lack of faith in him sliced through him like a surgeon's scalpel. He tightened his fingers around hers. "I *will* stop him, Clea."

"You don't have to convince me. I told you, I believe you."

The weight that had slammed like a two-ton boulder against his chest when she had spied that letter, shifted inside him making it easier for him to breathe again. "Will you be okay for a while while I make a few phone calls and check out the grounds around the apartment?"

"Sure. I'll be fine." She looked down at their joined hands. Then, as though suddenly realizing the intimacy their touch implied, she eased her fingers free. "Sorry I came apart on you earlier. That makes twice now that I've thrown myself into your arms wailing because I was scared. First at the theater and then again tonight."

"I'm not complaining."

"Yes, well…" She got to her feet, began fiddling with the ring on her finger as she prowled around the room. "…you should be. I haven't exactly been cooperative. And if I'd listened to you and installed that alarm like you suggested, tonight might have been avoided."

Ryan sighed at the change of subject. "No hindsight, Okay? Believe me, you'll only end up driving yourself crazy. Besides, I could have insisted you put in the alarm, but I didn't." But no question he should have, probably *would* have, if he had been thinking more about doing his job instead of falling in love with her.

The admission shocked him and sent that two-ton weight plummeting back on his chest faster than a landslide. He was in love with Clea. Canyon-deep, rock-solid, till-death-do-us-part love. The realization shook him, shook him right down to the soles of his feet. Until now, he had been sure when this mess was over he could walk away from her if she didn't want to pursue a relationship. A little bruised maybe, he admitted, but with no long-term damage. He'd only been kidding himself. When this was cleared up and that creep was behind bars, if Clea told him to take a hike, he wouldn't be damaged—he'd be flat-out destroyed.

Ryan dragged a hand through his hair and stood. Damn, he was trembling. His knees were the consistency of jelly. He hadn't been this rattled since the first time he had come up against a perp high on drugs and pointing an AK-47 at him. Come to think of it, he had been less shaken then.

"I mean it, Ryan. It's not your fault."

"All right. It's no one's fault." The truth was that if the guy had been determined to get in, he would have found a way no matter how good the alarm system was. And if his uncle was the one responsible for terrorizing Clea…Ryan shut off the thought. It couldn't be Uncle James. It couldn't.

"I'm going to see about having the thing installed in the morning."

"Good idea." His legs still unsteady, Ryan stood and pulled out his cell phone. He punched in the number for his brother Michael's pager and rubbed the tense muscles at the back of his neck. At the sound of the tone, he pressed in his number and hung up. Turning around, he watched

Clea check behind a chair, a table. "What are you looking for?"

"My briefcase. I want to make that note to call about the alarm."

"Your briefcase is still in the trunk of my car. I put it there before we went to Uncle Morgan's."

"Right. I forgot."

And forgetting work and her all-important calendar was something Clea seldom did, Ryan mused. He had learned that within the first two days he'd been with her. She was driven, focused, organized. So organized she could make an efficiency expert look inept. She was a woman with a plan. And that plan didn't include him. That realization slammed into him like a fist. How in the devil had love snuck up on him like this? And now that it had, what was he going to do about it? Somehow, unless he wanted to rip his heart out and leave it with her when this was over, he had to convince her he should be part of her plan.

The telephone rang. "It's probably Michael returning my call," he said, before answering the phone. After giving his brother a list of what needed to be done, he placed a call and left a message for the police officer in charge of Clea's case. Ending the call, he walked over to the edge of the path that she seemed so determined to wear in the carpet.

Eyes down, she was twisting the ring on her finger, but came to an abrupt stop when she noticed his size twelves in her way. "What?" she asked, her gaze darting up to his face. A tiny frown knitted itself across her forehead.

Foolish man that he was, he had the urge to smooth that crease on her brow with his finger. "You tell me. Why are you trying to make a permanent rut in this prissy white carpet of yours."

She glanced down at the floor in surprise, as though she had no idea that she had even been pacing, then shifted her gaze back up to him. "Guess I'm still a bit jumpy."

"A bit." He rubbed his hands up and down her arms.

"Try to relax. I'm going to dust for prints. When I finish, maybe you can take a bath or something. I've got Michael posting a twenty-four-hour guard on the apartment. The first shift should be here within the hour."

"But that'll cost—"

"The cost isn't important. You let me worry about it." If things went his way, he would claim the fee as a wedding gift. "One more thing. I think I should stay here in the apartment with you from now on."

"Why? Do you think he'll come back?"

He didn't want to frighten her, but was reluctant to lie. "He might. If he does, the man that'll be posted outside will probably scare him off. But if for some reason he makes it past my guy, I want to be close. I don't mind taking the couch."

"You don't have to. You can stay in the guest room."

Ryan nodded, pleased to have covered that hurdle so easily. "I'm waiting for a call back from Officer Delaney to report the break-in tonight. Then I'm going to want to talk to your neighbors, see if anyone saw or heard anything."

"I can give you a list," she offered as his phone rang a second time. While Ryan spoke to the police officer and filled him in, she put that nervous energy to work on the task he had given her.

By the time he hung up the phone a few minutes later, she had presented him with a neatly printed list of names. "The Tates live across the street, but they're in Boston visiting their new grandson right now. Ali Simpson lives on my left, but she's a flight attendant and travels a lot. I'm not sure if you'll catch her home. The Murphys on the right are newlyweds. You might have better luck with them."

"Thanks," Ryan said, tucking the sheet of paper in his pocket. "I'll be back in a few minutes. I'm going to check outside around the apartment. I'll bring you your briefcase in a couple of minutes. In the meantime, try not to touch anything in here until I can dust for prints.''

She followed him to the door. "Is there anything I can do?"

There was no mistaking the nerves still jumping around inside her, or the way she kept fiddling with the ring on her finger. "Just try to relax."

"I'm not very good at relaxing."

He'd noticed. But he didn't want her brooding over the situation either, so he scrambled for something he could give her to do to keep her mind off things. A thought came to mind, but he immediately dismissed it. She would have his head if he even suggested such a thing.

"What? What is it?" she demanded as though she'd read his thoughts. "Just give me a job. Anything. You want me to go talk to the neighbors?" She pounced on a pad of paper. "All right, just tell me what sort of questions to ask."

He caught her by the shoulders just to keep her still. "Clea, slow it down. I don't want you to question your neighbors. I need to do that."

"But what—"

"You've had a shock, and you're running on all engines. You keep going like this and you're going to burn yourself out."

She stiffened beneath his hands. Her head shot up. She looked him dead in the eye. "Despite my actions earlier, I'm not a wimp, Fitzpatrick."

"Never thought you were."

"Then don't treat me like one. I'm not some...some damsel in distress who needs to be rescued. I can take care of myself. And I want to do something besides sit here and twiddle my thumbs while you and the police do the work. Just give me a job to do, and I'll do it. You'll see."

It pleased him to see her feisty streak return. "Duchess, I don't doubt for a minute that you could do both my job and the police's job with your hands tied behind your back if you set your mind to it. But you're paying me to do a job, and you need to let me do it. My way. And I suspect the cops are going to want to handle their end of things, too."

She frowned at him. "So what am I supposed to do?"

"Well, there is one thing you could do, if you really want to," he said, knowing he was sticking his neck out by even suggesting it.

"What?"

"How about some dinner? I don't know about you, but I'm starving."

She blinked. "Cook?" she replied incredulously, making the word sound like one of the four-letter ones that had earned him a few mouth-washings and losses of privilege as a kid. "You want me to cook dinner for you?"

"Nothing fancy. A sandwich, some soup. Anything will do."

"A sandwich. Soup," she repeated.

Deciding he should scram while he still could, Ryan swooped down and stole a kiss. "Surprise me," he said against her shocked mouth, and slipped out the door before she went for his throat.

She'd never planned on fixing dinner for the sneaky man, Clea told herself. She'd had no intention of doing it whatsoever. At first the idea of the break-in, the sense of violation, had crowded her thoughts. The arrival of the police, and all the fussing over her by Sean and Michael, had kept her too busy to dwell on the fact that someone had been in her home. After Ryan had retrieved her briefcase, she dived into work. It hadn't helped. She just couldn't seem to concentrate. Even a soak in the tub hadn't helped to relax her.

But it wasn't thoughts of an intruder that had made her so restless, so distracted. It had been thoughts of Ryan. Or rather, her reaction to him. All sober and sharp-tongued, he had barked out orders to everyone with the precision of a marine drill sergeant. He'd made her feel safe. Safe, she thought with disgust. She'd never needed a man to make her feel safe before, never even wanted to. She was used to handling things on her own.

But with Ryan, it was different somehow. Whenever his gaze had strayed to her, there had been a warmth, a possessiveness in the way he'd looked at her that had calmed her, but had managed to stir up a whole new set of emotions. And those emotions had driven her into the kitchen.

"Aren't you going to eat any of the pizza?" he asked from across the dining room table.

Clea wrinkled her nose and took another sip of raspberry iced tea. "No. And I can't believe you're eating it."

"Wouldn't miss it. This is the first meal you've cooked for me," he told her as he bit into the charred, cardboard-like crust.

"And if you're lucky, it'll be the last."

He crunched down on the pitiful culinary mishap, and Clea winced. "It's really not that bad if you just scrape off some of the burned parts around the edges."

Clea leaned forward, pressed her fingertips to his forehead and shook her head. "No fever, so something must be wrong with your taste buds. The thing is awful, Ryan. Even I know that."

"You're being too hard on yourself," he told her as he sawed through another slice and started on it.

"I'm being honest. I told you I couldn't cook." She could run a business, go toe-to-toe with the best travel agency execs in town and hold her own without breaking a sweat, but when it came to domestic things—womanly, housewifely things—she was a complete failure. A flop. "I don't know what made me think I could make a pizza in the first place, except that the instructions on the box made it look so simple."

"Uh, next time you might want to follow the directions

without trying to improve on them. Although I think adding pesto and alfalfa sprouts was an interesting concept.''

The darn man was being sweet, she acknowledged, warmed by his response even though she tried not to be. ''Next time I want pizza, you can bet I'll pick up the phone and have the thing delivered.''

''That's up to you. But if you wanted to, I bet you could be a dynamite cook.''

''You say that after eating this disaster?''

''Sure,'' he told her as he began working on another slice. ''You forget, I've watched you work. You're smart. You're organized. You tackle a problem with the tenacity of a kid opening presents on Christmas morning. You know what you want, and you go after it. You don't give up. You're like a pit bull after a bone.''

''Gee, thanks.''

''What I'm saying is you're not a woman who scares easy. If I didn't already know that, you certainly proved it tonight.''

''Fitzpatrick, I'm afraid that pizza's done something to your brain. I came unglued tonight, remember?''

''You reacted the way any normal person would under the circumstances. Yeah, you were afraid for a couple of minutes. Who wouldn't be? But you didn't give in to that fear and fall apart like a lot of people would have done. The fact is, you don't run away from something that scares you. You face whatever it is head on and deal with it. It's one of the things I admire most about you.''

Except that they both knew she hadn't come close to dealing with her feelings for him. She looked down at the ring he had placed on her finger, recalled his offer to make the engagement a real one. She had been so tempted to accept his offer. He wanted her in a way that she didn't think any man ever could or would. And there was no question that she wanted him. But she'd been afraid. Afraid of the hurt that she knew would come when Ryan realized what a fraud she was, and moved on. She had survived one disastrous love affair that had come very close to breaking her. Something told her if she took a chance on Ryan and failed, she would never come out of it whole. No way was she as brave as he believed her to be. "I appreciate the vote of confidence. But I think I'll limit my challenges to business in the future and leave the domestic front to my two sisters."

He was disappointed in her, she could see it in his eyes, feel it and was struck by how much that hurt. He put away another two pieces of the pizza in silence, then stood. "Since you cooked, I'll do the cleanup."

"Sounds fair."

But she helped him anyway. Within minutes they had the counters wiped clean, the dishes loaded in the dishwater, and Ryan had just served himself a cup of coffee.

"Since you've suffered so gallantly through that debacle of a meal and even pretended to enjoy it—"

"I did enjoy it."

"If you say so. Anyway, I have a surprise for you."

He arched an eyebrow. "What sort of surprise?"

"Something that will make up for the pizza, I hope. You just sit there. I'll be right back." Retreating to the freezer, she whipped out the two banana splits she had created with ice cream, an over-ripe banana, some chopped nuts and a jar of chocolate sauce she had hidden for emergencies. She topped off the diet disasters with two cherries each and carried them into the dining room.

"Ta da!" She set them on the table with a flourish.

"You made this?" he asked, all but drooling over the lip-smacking dessert.

"With my own two little hands."

"This looks fantastic," he said, approaching the masterpiece with reverence. He put a monster-size spoonful of chocolate sauce, banana and vanilla ice cream into his mouth, closed his eyes and groaned. Then he dug in for another bite.

Clea laughed. "Fitzpatrick, you're such a hedonist. If you ever looked at me like that I'd run for the hills."

His gazed skipped up to her face, and Clea's heart jumped at the hungry look he slid over her. "Then you might want to start running," he said with a smile that had her pulse spiking and her heart pounding like a drum.

He polished off his banana split at breathtaking speed and then began eyeing hers. "You going to eat all of that?" he asked, aiming his spoon toward the thick drizzle of chocolate syrup spreading over her mound of ice cream.

"Yes, I am." Clea tugged her dish closer to her. "And unless you have a death wish, I'd recommend you keep that spoon on your side of the table."

Ryan chuckled. "Serious about our ice cream, are we?"

"Dead serious," she told him, and savored another bite. "My sisters will tell you, I've been known to become violent when someone tries swiping my dessert."

"Violent, huh?" he asked, just before dipping his spoon into her dish and stealing a chunk of banana.

She scowled at him and threatened to tell his brothers he liked tofu, and preferred herbal tea to beer.

He hesitated at that one. "You play dirty, Duchess."

"I play to win."

"So do I," he said, his voice suddenly soft, determined, serious.

Clea's gaze met his. The laughter died on her lips. There was no mistaking the dark fire in his eyes. They were no longer talking about desserts, and she knew it. She swallowed, but the air in her lungs seemed to suddenly grow shallow. Quickly, she stood. "It's getting late. I'd better get ready for bed. I have a busy day tomorrow."

Ryan stood, too. He carried his dish to the sink. "Thanks for dinner."

"You're welcome," she said, drying her hands before

following him into the living room. After he had checked with the man he had posted outside, he came back inside and followed her down the hall to the guest bedroom.

Clea zipped through the room, showing him where the blankets, towels and soap were kept. "I think you should be able to find everything you need," she told him, exiting the bedroom faster than a kitten scrambling after a ball of yarn.

"Looks like it."

Her heart pounded at the sudden intimacy of standing with him in the semi-darkness outside her bedroom. She could smell the scent of soap and male, see the dark whiskers shadowing his jaw. She was keenly aware of the size and power in him. And she wanted.... She hadn't thought any man could make her feel those things again. Yet, Ryan did. "Well, good night," she finally managed to say, and started to turn away.

Ryan touched her cheek, staying her movement. And as she watched, he dipped his head and brushed his mouth across hers so gently it was barely a whisper. Her eyes fluttered closed at the drugging effect of his soft caresses. She parted her lips, and his tongue slipped inside to dance with hers. Her senses began to spin. He tasted of chocolate and coffee, of loneliness and longing. He tugged at the loneliness inside her, the longings she had buried years ago and had sworn never to give in to again. Yet, she was powerless to stop the sensations swimming inside her. Sensations like none she had ever known before. She could feel the thudding of his heart beneath her fingertips, feel his arousal pressed hard and heavy against her belly. Dangerous. He was much too dangerous, she told herself and forced herself to end the kiss.

Their ragged breathing echoed in the silent hallway. Her heart was still racing like a young filly. Slowly, she opened her eyes, and as her vision began to clear, all she could see was his face.

"How long are you going to make us wait, Clea?" he asked in a voice that was as dark and savage as his expression.

"Ryan, please don't. I've told you, I don't want to have an affair with you." She started for her bedroom.

Ryan followed her, caught her before she could open the door. "I've offered you a hell of a lot more than an affair," he reminded her.

"I know. But we both know it was your hormones talking."

"Maybe that's the way it was in the beginning. A man would have to be a monk to look at you and not want you, and I've never claimed to be a monk."

"No," she said, trying to lighten the mood with a smile. "We both know you're not a monk."

"And I've never claimed to be a saint either. But there haven't been as many women as you probably think. I haven't been involved with anyone for more than a year. If you want me to take one of those tests—"

"I believe you," she said, realizing how important it was to him that she believe him.

"Then believe me when I tell you that you're special, Clea. I've never wanted anyone the way I want you. And it's not just sex. I want to spend my life with you. I—"

She put her fingers against his mouth. "Please, Ryan, don't."

"Why not?"

"Because you don't know me. I'm not the woman you think I am. I can't be the woman you want me to be."

"The woman you are is the only woman I want. I love you, and I think you love me, too."

Clea squeezed her eyes shut a moment, feeling as though her heart were being ripped in two. Heaven help her, she did love him. Too much to sentence him to a life with a woman who could only be half a wife. He deserved more. She wanted him to have more. Opening her eyes, she deliberately made her voice hard, cold as she said, "You're wrong, Ryan. I'm attracted to you physically, yes. But that's all."

"You're lying," he said, his voice sharp, his expression dark and furious.

She shrugged. "Believe what you want, but it's the truth. You don't fit into my plans. The most important thing to me is seeing that Destinations succeeds. Once I buy out your aunt and uncle, I'm going to turn it into the best travel agency in Chicago."

"And what about your personal life? Is owning that damn agency going to satisfy you in bed at night? Hold you close and make love to you?"

Clea swallowed past the painful lump lodged in her throat and looked him square in the eye. "The agency's all I want or need," she lied. "If you can't handle that and do the job I hired you to do, tell me now, and I'll get someone who can," she said being deliberately cruel.

Ryan stepped back as though she had slapped him. Black fire burned in his eyes. "Don't worry, Duchess, I can handle the job."

And as he walked away, Clea clutched her arms around her middle, feeling as though he had just cut out a piece of her heart and taken it with him.

Eight

Hours later, he still couldn't sleep. No surprise in that, Ryan told himself as he kicked off the covers and sat up in bed. Once he'd cooled off and had had time to think, he'd realized it had all been an act on Clea's part. The short of it was she'd lied to him. He was sure of it. But the question that kept nagging at him was why. Why did she want him to believe she was some cold, calculating business shark who cared more about bottom lines and profits than about people? Despite what she had said, she did care about him. So why did she keep pushing him away? It just didn't make any sense.

He glanced at the clock on the bedside table. Barely 3:00 in the morning, he noted, but got up anyway and wandered to the window. The sky was pitch black, the moon hidden by a veil of thick clouds. Morning was still hours away. Not that it mattered. Sleep didn't seem to be an option for him because every time he closed his eyes, thoughts of Clea, images of her, continued to play in his head.

And he had no one to blame but himself, Ryan chided. He never should have gone to her bedroom. But he had heard her tossing and turning, murmuring something in her sleep, and had eased open her door to check on her, just to make sure she was all right.

Big mistake, Ryan admitted, washing a hand over his face. He had still been aching from that kiss they had shared earlier. Not her rejection, nor a cold shower nor the latest thriller by his favorite author had been able to obliterate the burning hunger inside him. Seeing her lying in the center of that big soft-looking bed, all sleep-tousled and tempting in some silky white thing, had nearly brought him to his knees. He'd wanted her—which was no big surprise. He'd been wanting Clea from the moment he'd first set eyes on her. And he doubted any man with a pulse could look at her and not feel that bite of desire.

But it was more than desire this time. More than sex. Much more. Because for the first time that he could remember, he wanted more than mutually satisfying sex with a woman. He wanted to make love to her, with her. To lose himself in her, have her lose herself in him. And he wanted them to go on losing and finding in each other. He wanted a life with Clea. A life with all the sappy, wonderful things that went with it—marriage and commitment, white picket fences and mortgage payments, diapers and braces. Ryan laughed at himself as he thought of his brothers and their reaction to that. But it was true. He wanted all those joys and headaches that made up a marriage, that made up two people sharing a life together. And he wanted them with Clea.

The problem was convincing her that she wanted them, too. He thought about her lying in the bed just in the next room, so soft and beautiful, and breathed deeply as his body responded to those thoughts. Best to think about something else, he decided, or else he was in for another cold shower.

Restless, he slipped on his jeans and a shirt, and went out to check with the operative posted outside.

Fifteen minutes later, satisfied the guy had everything under control, he headed back to the apartment. He had just unlocked the door when he heard the telephone ringing. Ryan dashed across the room and snatched up the receiver, hoping to reach it before Clea did. But he was too late.

"Did you get my note?" came the ragged whisper, and something familiar about it gnawed at Ryan.

"Stop it! Why are you doing this to me? Why do you keep calling me? Sending me those awful letters?"

Something tore at him as he heard the panic in Clea's voice. He slammed down the phone and headed at a run for her bedroom.

"Please, please just leave me alone."

Ryan grabbed the receiver from Clea's fingers.

"I can't. Don't you see, I can't," the man insisted and then started to weep. "I love you. I love you so much."

"But the lady doesn't love you, pal."

Ryan heard the gasp.

"No! That's not true! She loves me. I know she does."

"Wrong. She loves me. She's going to marry me."

There was a cry of rage followed by a string of foul words. For a second, for the briefest of seconds, Ryan thought he caught something in the voice again. But before he could grasp it, the line went dead.

Ryan clicked twice and waited for his man to come on. "Did you get a location?"

"Another pay phone. This time at the airport."

Which meant even if the number wasn't scrambled again, it would be almost impossible to trace who had placed that call. "Check it out anyway," Ryan ordered, then replaced the receiver in its cradle.

He glanced over at Clea. Soft light spilled from the ginger-jar lamp on the bedside table, illuminating the small, delicate figure huddled amidst a tumble of navy satin sheets. She sat in the middle of the four-poster bed, hugging her arms around her legs, her head bowed, her face buried against her knees. "Are you all right?"

"Yes," she said, her voice muffled and thick with tears. "I'll be okay. I just need a couple of minutes alone."

But he couldn't leave her alone. Not like this. The fist squeezing his heart tightened. He felt helpless, frustrated and angry with himself for not saving her from this. She wouldn't be like this right now, he told himself, had he not broken the cardinal rule of a bodyguard—falling in love with the woman he had been hired to protect. He had known better. Michael had even tried to warn him. But he hadn't listened. He had been so sure he could keep a handle on his feelings and protect her at the same time. Instead, he had lost his objectivity and had failed her. He had missed something important. Something he shouldn't have missed, *wouldn't* have missed, if he had been focused as he should have been. And now Clea was paying the price for his failure.

He would make it up to her, he vowed silently. He was going to find this jerk and put an end to his terrorizing her if it was the last thing he did. Her soft sobs cut another chunk out of him. Unable to stand it any longer, he sat down on the bed beside her and drew her into his arms. "It's okay. It's okay."

She clung to him, wept on his shoulder. Ryan didn't know how long he held her, whispering softly, stroking his hand up and down her back while she cried out all her tears. When the storm finally passed, he set her from him and tipped up her chin. Her eyes were wet and bright with tears. Big fat drops rolled down her cheeks and chin. Retrieving his handkerchief from his pocket, he mopped up the tears that remained. "Feel better?" he asked, pressing the handkerchief into her palm and closing her fingers over it.

"Yes. Thank you."

"Any time. Want me to get you something to drink? Some milk? Hot tea? Something to help you get back to sleep. Just name it, and it's yours."

"I don't want anything to drink."

He eased away from her a fraction. "Then I guess I'd better let you try to get some rest. I'm sure you've got a busy day planned."

"I don't want to go to sleep. And I don't want to think about work," she murmured as her eyes met his.

The air between them vibrated. Ryan felt the awareness sizzling, scorching him with its heat. "What do you want, Clea?"

"You."

Ryan's heart thundered in his chest. He swallowed. "I want you so much right now, it hurts just to breathe. But not like this. Not when you're scared and vulnerable. It wouldn't be fair to either of us."

"I'm not a schoolgirl, Ryan. I know what I'm doing. I know what I want. And I want you." She slipped her arms up his chest, sending arrows of heat shooting through his body. "Make love to me, Ryan. Make love to me and make me forget that there were ever any phone calls, that there were ever any letters. Make love to me until all I can remember, all I can think about, is you."

Reaching up, she pressed her mouth against his. It was the sweet, slow kiss of a temptress. A kiss of hunger. A kiss of need. For a second, a fraction of a second at best, Ryan held himself back, grappled for control.

But then she traced his lips, moving that wet, pink tongue across the seam of his mouth, and the last of his control snapped. Heat exploded inside him. Every nerve in his body short-circuited. Every pulse zapped to life. His hands somehow found themselves fisting, tangling in her hair, and he pulled her close, closer, closer still.

He tore his mouth free long enough to drag in a breath and try to regain his sanity.

"Make love to me," she whispered.

Sanity be damned, he decided and dipped his head down for another taste. One kiss spun into another, and then another. Hot, wet kisses that devoured and fed. He could kiss her for hours, Ryan thought. For days. For a lifetime.

Clea tugged her mouth free. "Touch me, Ryan. Please."

She didn't have to ask him twice. He slid his fingers down her throat, palmed the curve of her breasts, glided along the arc of her waist. He cupped her bottom and then retraced his journey, molding, caressing, exploring. She was silk and steel beneath his hands, sweetness and sin. And she was slowly driving him mad with those soft sighs she was making. He wanted her fast and hard, slow and sweet. He drove his tongue into her mouth.

Her tongue dueled with his. She attacked the buttons on his shirt and sent them scattering to the floor. She jerked her mouth free and looked up at him with eyes glazed with desire. "I want to feel you against me," she said on a jagged breath before pressing her lips to his chest.

Ryan nearly came off the bed at the feel of her hot, wet mouth on his skin. He yanked his shirt off and before it hit the floor, her hands were on him again, racing over his shoulders and down his chest to the snap on his jeans. He sucked in a breath as her fingers went to work on his zipper.

Groaning, Ryan whipped the piece of sinful silk off her and tossed it to the floor. His breath caught at the sight of her naked body before him. Full, firm breasts with rosy-tipped nipples pebbled against his fingertips.

She arched her back, filling his palms with her sweet-smelling flesh.

Ryan kicked off his jeans, dragged her body against his and kissed her again. It was erotic. Her soft, warm skin pressed against his hard, muscled flesh. It was intoxicating. It was driving him to the edge of control. He dragged his mouth free, trying to slow down the fever burning in his blood like a wildfire. He nipped at her stubborn chin, tasted the hollow in her throat, licked and suckled the rosy peaks of her breasts. But instead of slowing down, the sweet noises coming from her only made the fire in him burn hotter, faster.

Somewhere he heard a dog bark. A radio click on. Her throaty moan. The blood roared in his ears, sizzled in his veins. He swallowed those soft, little sounds coming from her lips and feasted on that luscious mouth. Emotions slammed through him, hitting him hard and fast. Desire, need, tenderness, love.

Her fingers found him, closed around him and Ryan groaned.

"I want to feel you inside me," she murmured.

And it was where he wanted to be. He yanked off the lace covering her and moved between her thighs. A tiny thread of sanity remained, and he grappled for the item he had remembered to remove from his jeans. He found the packet, ripped it open with his teeth.

"Let me help."

His body shook when she smoothed the sheath over him. And then he couldn't wait any longer. Need grabbed him by the throat until he could barely breathe. He entered her in one, deep, long stroke.

She gasped his name, and Ryan struggled to hold back, afraid for a moment that he had hurt her. But then she was arching her back, her nails biting into his skin, as her body moved with his and she took him deeper inside her.

He gave her everything, but held himself back, waiting, watching, wanting to see her face when the first climax hit her, wanting to hear his name on her lips as it did.

"Ryan," she cried out as the climax slammed into her, made her shudder in his arms.

Ryan latched his mouth onto hers, devouring her with his tongue and teeth as he drove himself harder, faster, deeper inside her. And when he felt her begin to shudder again, felt his body shatter as the climax hit him, he tore his mouth free and whispered, "I love you."

Clea awoke to the sound of running water and Ryan singing at the top of his lungs in her shower. She shifted to pull the comforter up over her and was struck by aches in places that she hadn't even realized could hurt.

She squeezed her eyes shut a moment and thought back on those wild, crazy hours she'd spent in Ryan's arms. She thought she'd known what to expect from sex. She wasn't a young virgin without any sexual experience as she'd been the last time she had an affair. But nothing in her relationship with Eric Ramsey had prepared her for making love with Ryan. There had been nothing tame and soft about their coming together. He'd been rough and demanding. So had she. Clea cringed as she recalled her hungry response to him.

And he'd told her he loved her.

"It's a little late for regrets."

Clea's eyes popped open, and her gaze darted to the bathroom door. Ryan stood in the doorway, a towel draped low on his hips and his hair damp from his shower, as steam billowed around him. "Who said I have regrets?"

He narrowed his eyes. "Don't you?"

"No." She didn't have any regrets. What was the point? Besides, how could she regret what had been the most incredible experience of her life? "You said yourself, we're both adults. If we choose to have an affair, I don't see where it's anyone's business but our own."

"An affair. Is that how you see what's happening between us?"

"Don't you?"

Ryan made his way to her bed. "No," he told her as he peeled back the covers and devoured her with his eyes. "An affair doesn't even come close to describing what's happening between us. What I want to happen between us."

Clea's heart began to stammer as he stripped the towel from his waist and joined her in the bed. His arousal pressed hard and heavy and hot against her as he propped himself up on his elbow to look at her. She wanted him again, she realized as her blood began to heat. She wanted that wild, crazy free fall that she experienced only when he was with her, inside her. "I don't want to argue."

"That makes two of us," he told her as he positioned himself between her thighs. "I don't want to argue either."

Anticipation beat like a drumroll in her veins as he dipped his head to nip at her mouth, her throat, her breasts. "Then don't. Let's just enjoy this…" She squirmed at the feel of his teeth on her sensitized flesh as his mouth closed over first one nipple and then the other.

"This what?" he murmured as his mouth traveled to her stomach and down farther to kiss the inside of her thighs.

"This chemistry between us," she managed to get out before he moved between her thighs and loved her with his mouth. His tongue tasted her, loved her until she thought surely she would shatter.

When the climax ripped into her at the speed of light, she cried out. Ryan caught her hands, meshed his fingers with hers. "All right, Duchess, we'll do this your way for now," he whispered as he moved up between her thighs. "But I'm warning you, I have no intention of ever letting you go."

And before she could protest, tell him he was wrong, he drove into her and sent them both spiraling through sky and space until they exploded amidst the stars.

"Earth to Clea."

Clea jumped at the sound of her name. "I'm sorry, Gayle. Did you say something?"

The other woman laughed. "Boy, does she have it bad. I guess that's what love does to you, huh?"

"I guess so," Ryan said as he watched the flush crawl up Clea's cheeks. Even after spending every night for a week in the same bed, making love to her, trying to show her how much he loved her, he was no closer to convincing Clea that what they shared was more than sex. He had promised himself to give her time, to wait until his investigation was cleared up, but each day as the investigation was stymied, he grew more impatient for Clea to admit that what they shared was real. He loved her and wanted to marry her, spend his life with her. But except when they were in bed together, she remained as skittish as a colt. In the meantime his family was champing at the bit to host an engagement party. So far, he'd held them off, but there had been no getting out of attending the christening for one of his Donatelli cousins on the West Coast. A grand celebration had been planned at the family's vineyard estate and everyone was eager to meet Clea.

"Very funny," Clea said. "Now, what was it you wanted to know?" she asked her assistant.

"Whether or not you'd like me to make an appointment for you to view a few of the resorts while you're in Napa Valley for the christening this weekend."

"That's *this* weekend?" Clea asked.

"Yes," Gayle told her. "It's on your calendar. And since Charlotte Don Levy called herself asking for us to quote on the firm's retreat, I thought you might want to scout out a few sights. I know you've always wanted to scoop Ramsey Travel and land the Don Levy account for Destinations. Thought this might be your chance."

"Yes, please. Go ahead and see what you can set up."

After her assistant left, Ryan closed the door. Temper simmered inside him. Part frustration, part annoyance, he admitted, because he had recognized the name of the other agency and its owner. Jealousy sank its teeth into him as he recalled his early inquiries turning up the name Eric Ramsey, and Clea's affair with the man six years ago. "We're going to California for a family christening, not to conduct business."

"I didn't mean for you to miss out on spending time with your family, Ryan. I don't need you to go with me. I can check out the resorts on my own."

Her remark sent his temper shooting up another notch. Placing his hands flat on her desk, he leaned over until his face was within inches of hers. "Let's get something straight, Duchess. As far as anyone knows, we're engaged. That means my family is your family."

"Ryan, I plan to go with you to the christening," she argued.

"You'll do more than go to the christening. You're going to spend time with me. With my family. With the family you're supposed to be marrying into."

"You and I both know—"

"This isn't negotiable. This weekend belongs to us."

Defiance sparked in her eyes. "I have a business to run. Just because the two of us are having an affair—"

"Don't toss that word out at me unless you're prepared to deal with the consequences because you and I both know there's more than sex going on between us."

When she didn't fight him on that, he worked at keeping a lid on his temper and continued, "Now, if you want to hang around in California for a couple of extra days to check out some resorts, we can do that. I just didn't realize you were so eager to thumb your nose at your old lover by stealing one of his plum accounts."

Clea gasped. Her face turned white, but she recovered quickly. "For the record, the Don Levy account was mine. I was the one who brought it to the Ramsey Agency in the first place."

"What's going on, Clea?"

"I told you, the Don Levy account—"

"I don't give a damn about the account. I mean why does my mentioning the name Eric Ramsey make you turn white?"

"I...I didn't realize you knew anything about my, about my relationship with him. How did you find out?"

"It turned up when I was digging for possible suspects."

"You never mentioned it."

"Didn't see any point since I ruled him out as a suspect. Apparently, Ramsey's last wife kicked him out for having an affair with their kids' au pair, and he's spent most of his time during the past six months in France, trying to get her back to the States."

"His poor wife."

"I wouldn't feel so sorry for her. Word has it, she'll probably end up with the agency."

"Good for her," Clea said. Some color came back into her cheeks. "Maybe I won't go after the Don Levy account after all."

"That's up to you." But the green-eyed monster still had its teeth in him. "You still got a thing for Ramsey? That why you looked like you'd seen a ghost when I mentioned his name?"

"Put a lid on the testosterone, Fitzpatrick. I'm not carrying any torches for Eric Ramsey. I'm just ashamed to admit that I was once gullible and stupid enough to fall for the man's lies, and have an affair with him."

"You were a kid," he pointed out. "He was older, sophisticated and, from what I've been told, very smooth."

"Oh, he was smooth all right. He forgot to explain, when he told me he and his wife were separated, that he meant she was on a tour of Europe with their daughter and still very much his wife."

"The scum!"

"When I found that out I.... When I went to him with the truth, he never denied it. That's when I left the agency, my dream job and started over."

Ryan came around the desk and pulled her into his arms. "Want me to break him in two for you?"

"No. But thanks anyway."

"Any time," he told her, stealing a kiss.

"Ahem. Excuse me."

Ryan looked up at the sound of his uncle's voice, caught the worried look in the other man's eye. "What can we do for you, Uncle James?"

The older man shoved a nervous hand through his graying hair. "Sorry to interrupt. But I was wondering if I could have a private word with Clea for a moment."

"Of course, James. Ryan was just leaving. Weren't you, Ryan?"

He wanted to object. This wasn't the first time his uncle had needed a private word with Clea. In fact, those private chats seemed to be becoming more and more frequent. And when he questioned Clea as to the reason behind them, she either gave him some drivel about business or, when he told her he wasn't buying it, clammed up all together.

"I'm going, but I want something to hold me over." He took her mouth in a hot, greedy kiss. Not until he felt her resistance crumble, until he felt her quiver in his arms, did he end the kiss and release her.

And as he pulled the office door shut behind him, Ryan caught the yearning expression on his uncle's face. It made him feel as though he had just been kicked in the stomach and left an acid taste in his mouth. He thought of the man who had taken him to baseball games, the man who had taught him how to change the line on his fishing pole. Then he remembered the same man who had gone on a month-long drinking binge when his wife had left him. The man who had stalked his wife and been arrested before he had hit rock bottom and entered a rehab program. His uncle had licked his problem and won back Aunt Maggie. But what if he'd developed a new obsession? And what if that new obsession was Clea?

Nine

"**A**nd this lovely creature is my soon-to-be daughter-in-law Clea. She's going to marry my Ryan," Isabel Fitzpatrick proclaimed proudly to yet another bevy of Donatellis at the christening party.

"Hello," Clea said, accepting what had to be the hundredth hug and welcoming kiss to the family. She felt like such a fraud, smiling, accepting this family's affection and good wishes, when she knew in her heart her engagement to Ryan could never be real.

"When's the wedding?" one of Ryan's cousins asked.

"And how soon before you two start making little Fitzpatricks?"

Clea blinked at the elderly Aunt Sarah—Donatelli or Fitzpatrick, she couldn't remember which. "I...um...Ryan and I haven't discussed it."

"Well, if I know my nephew, you'll have a house full," the other woman declared and everyone broke into laughter.

"Excuse me, ladies," Ryan said, materializing at her side. "Mind if I steal my future bride for a dance?"

Without waiting for their approval, Ryan whisked her away and onto the dance floor. When the music slowed, he led her out onto the veranda. "Thanks," she said, wrapping the amethyst scarf she had worn around her bare shoulders.

"My pleasure. Feeling better now?"

"Was I that obvious?"

He grinned, flashing that Fitzpatrick dimple at her. "You looked like you were about to face a firing squad."

"I guess I was a bit overwhelmed."

"Perfectly understandable," he told her, swiping two glasses of wine from a waiter's tray and handing one of them to her. "To families," he said, tapping her glass in a toast.

"To families," Clea repeated and took a sip of the wine, pleased to discover it was more of the family's prizewinning cabernet sauvignon.

"So, how are you holding up?"

"You tell me," Clea said, beginning to relax a little.

"I think you're doing great. The family loves you."

"Which one?" Clea asked jokingly, noting the huge numbers of people filling the gigantic house and spilling out onto the veranda.

Ryan leaned back against the railing. "We are quite a handful, aren't we?"

Clea chuckled. "I'd say a handful is a bit of an understatement."

He grinned. "You're right. More like major overload with both families here. But I hope you're having a good time in spite of us."

"Oh, I am," Clea assured him. "Your family's wonderful. You're very lucky."

"What about your family? I know you have two sisters. Any brothers, hoards of cousins?"

"We're a small lot compared to you guys. I have two

aunts, three uncles and an assortment of cousins. I've also got a niece or nephew on the way," she said with a smile, thinking of Lorelei's pregnancy. She was thrilled for her sister, but couldn't help feeling a pang of longing, regret.

"So, do you see them often?" Ryan asked, cutting into her thoughts.

"Not really. We're close, but not the way your family is. Since my folks are in showbiz, we tended to move around a lot, and I guess you could say we're sort of scattered now. But when we do get together it's wonderful."

Growing more relaxed, Clea found herself telling him funny stories from her childhood, about her parents' aspirations for their daughters to be in the movies and how they named the girls after sirens of the screen. Of how her own curiosity and sense of adventure to learn everything she could about each new place they had called home had led to her desire to go into the travel business. She was just finishing up the story of her combined debut and finale as part of a dance troupe when a sudden chill chased down her spine.

"What is it?" Ryan asked.

Suddenly uneasy, Clea hugged her scarf around her like a shield. "I don't know. I just had this strange feeling, like I'm being watched."

"Probably because you are. Not that it's all that surprising since you're the most beautiful woman here," he told her. He put his arm around her, but she hadn't missed his alert stance or the way his eyes scanned the trees and shrubs beyond the deck to the valley stretched out below.

"Hey, Ry. Dad's looking for you," Sean called out from the doorway. Ryan hesitated.

"Go ahead. I'll be fine," Clea assured him. "I'm just going to stay out here for a little while."

He dropped a quick kiss on her lips. "I won't be long."

Setting her half-full wineglass down on a table, Clea turned her back on the party and glanced out at the expanse of gardens and trees sweeping before her. With the temperate climate, roses splashed the garden with red, yellow and white, scenting the air with their sweet smell. Beyond the gardens and shrubbery, redwood trees towered in the sky. She thought of the vineyards that spread over acres and acres of Donatelli land—land that had been in Ryan's family for generations. It was part of his heritage. A heritage that he would want to continue. A heritage that he could never continue with her.

Emotions swirled through her. She loved him. So much, so very much that she ached with it. She pressed a fist to her heart and blinked back the threatening tears. And because she loved him, she had to let him go.

"Aha, got you alone at last."

Clea nearly jumped at the sound of Sean's voice. Swallowing, she schooled her expression before turning to face him. She forced a smile. "I wouldn't exactly say we're alone," she told him, her gaze indicating the dozen or so others who had wandered outside.

Sean flashed her his breath-stealing grin. "Guess you're right," he said, handing her a fresh glass of wine. "But it looks like you were having some mighty deep thoughts. You okay? I know things have been going pretty fast for you, what with that problem you've been having and you and Ryan getting engaged and all. Some pretty heavy stuff."

"Yes, it is," she replied, wishing she hadn't let Ryan talk her into keeping even his brothers in the dark about them. "But I'm fine. Really." But once again she felt uneasy, struck by that sense that she was being watched.

"Looking for someone?" he asked, obviously noting her eyes wandering the deck.

"No. Not really." She shook her head and took a sip of wine. "I just keep getting the strangest feeling someone is watching me."

"You mean someone besides me, my brothers and every other man in the place?"

Clea chuckled. "You sound just like Ryan. Tell me, do the women usually fall for this malarkey you fellows dole out?"

He gave her a wounded look, put a hand to his chest. "Darling, obviously my baby brother has shown you none of the legendary Fitzpatrick charm. Want me to have a talk with him?"

"That's all right," Clea told him, enjoying the silly exchange in spite of the heavy feeling in her heart. It was strange. She had known Sean for years and liked him. He was every bit as handsome as Ryan. They shared the same dark good looks, the Viking cheekbones, those incredible blue eyes. Even the Fitzpatrick dimple was the same. No question about it, Sean Fitzpatrick was a bonafide hunk. The number of single females that had been buzzing around him all evening only affirmed that opinion. Yet Sean didn't make her heart beat faster or her body hum with desire the way Ryan did.

"Ah, now that's music a man can dance to," he said as the band struck up the first notes of "Danny Boy." Taking Clea's glass from her fingers, Sean set it aside and was just reaching for her when Ryan clamped a hand on his shoulder.

"Get your mitts off her. You want to dance, find your own girl," Ryan told him. "This one's mine."

Sean shot Ryan a disgusted look and turned back to Clea. He gave her another once-over and, sighing with obvious regret, he released her. "Just as I suspected, darling. My baby brother here missed out on the Fitzpatrick charm."

"Keep looking at her like that, and I'm gonna have to feed you those pretty white teeth that you're always flashing at the ladies," Ryan countered, fire sparking in his eyes.

Sean made a face. "No charm and nasty tempered, too.

Sure you want to marry this guy instead of me? It's not too late to change your mind, you know.''

Ryan took a step toward his brother and Clea neatly slipped her arm through his before fists started to fly. "I appreciate the offer, Sean,'' she said smoothly, tugging Ryan's stiff body closer to hers. "But I think I'll keep him. Come on, Ryan. Dance with me?''

"Are you going to keep me, Clea?'' he asked as he led her to the center of the veranda and took her into his arms.

Oh, how she wanted to keep him, she admitted silently. But not wanting to ruin the moment, she pressed her finger against his lips and whispered, "If I could stop time at a moment and place where I had everything I wanted, where I was happiest and would want to spend the rest of eternity, that moment would be now. Here. In your arms.''

Ryan's eyes shimmered with a savage heat and hunger that stole her breath away. His gaze pounced on her, touching her everywhere—her eyes, her mouth, her throat, her breasts. Desire had never been like this before. So powerful. So thrilling. He moved her around in a slow circle beneath the twinkling lights and ribbon streamers draped above the deck. A late September breeze stirred and sent her scarf whispering across her shoulders. Ryan pressed a kiss to her bare skin, and she shivered.

Glasses clinked, champagne corks popped. Someone squealed. Laughter rang out around them. Clea scarcely heard any of it as Ryan urged her body closer and swept her into another slow spin.

She could feel the beat of his heart under her palm where her fingers had stolen beneath his jacket. She could feel the brush of his thigh, the weight and heat of his erection, as he continued to dance her around the veranda. The music played on, switching to a bluesy tune with a wailing sax, and then to another song with a heated rhythm and ascending drumbeat that echoed the quickening beat of her heart, the desire vibrating inside her.

"I want you," Ryan told her, his voice raw and harsh, his eyes dark with need.

"And I want you."

She didn't need to say anything more. Grabbing her hand, Ryan extended a flurry of quick, almost curt good-byes to his family. Ignoring the amused expressions at their hasty departure, he hustled her down the stairs of the Donatellis' main house and outside to retrieve the snazzy silver convertible he had insisted on renting.

She should have been embarrassed, Clea told herself as they waited for the car to be brought around. And she would have been—except that she was as eager for him as he seemed to be for her. The realization shocked her, frightened her a little. How had a woman who'd remained celibate for the past six years suddenly become such a wanton creature? While she would have liked to blame it on hormones, she knew that wasn't the case. It was Ryan. She had thought she'd known passion before, thought she'd known love. She realized now she had never even had a clue about either.

Not until Ryan had come into her life. Before Ryan she had not truly known how wonderful life could be. And when things ended between them, and he was gone, how would she ever go back to her life without him?

That was a problem she would have to deal with, Clea told herself. But later. Not now. Now she would take what special moments were left to them and enjoy them while she still could.

The car came to a stop before her, and Clea lifted the long flowing skirts of her strapless dress and eased into her seat. Her fingers trembled as she pulled the silk scarf up over her hair, draped the ends loosely across her throat and over her shoulders to trail down her back. She reached for her seat belt, fumbled with the catch.

"Clea."

Her gaze met his, and the ends of the seat belt tangled in her lap.

He leaned over, cupped her face in his hands and kissed her. The kiss was whisper-soft, tender, and filled with a desperate yearning that made her heart catch in her chest. When he lifted his lips from hers, he said, "I love you."

Car lights flashed behind them, and Ryan sent the convertible speeding down the curving road. They drove in silence mile after mile, winding along the tree-lined road. The sky stretched out before them, a dusty canvas sprinkled with lights. The wind whispered against her skin, pressing cool autumn kisses to her face and mouth, and sending the ends of her scarf dancing behind her.

Ryan turned the steering wheel and pointed the car onto a dirt road that took them through row after row of lush green vines heavy with the scent of ripe grapes. She didn't ask him where they were going. She didn't care. Not as long as she was with him.

By the time he pulled the car to a stop next to a large pond, awareness was singing between them, the drumbeat of desire louder and higher with each note. Within moments, he had retrieved a blanket from the trunk of the car and was taking her hand, leading her to a grove of trees. As he spread the blanket beneath the trees, Clea watched him.

He had left his jacket in the car, along with his tie. His white shirt spread across wide shoulders, the open collar giving teasing glimpses of bronzed skin and dark hair. He lowered himself to the blanket, kicked off his shoes and held out his hand. "Make love with me, Clea."

The deep raw sound of his voice touched her like a caress. But it was his eyes, those intense silver-blue eyes, dark with need and love, mirroring his uncertainty of her response, that made her tremble with longing. Taking his hand, she knelt down beside him.

He touched her as though she were spun glass, gently

loosening the scarf that lay puddled around her shoulders. "You're so beautiful," he told her, capturing her face in his hands. He kissed her brow, her cheek, her chin. Kisses that appeased, yet tempted.

She knew he could be tender, knew he could be gentle. But she didn't want tender or gentle now. She didn't want slow—not when this fire-hot need burned inside her for him. Curling her fingers in his hair, she yanked his mouth until it was only a breath from her own. "Kiss me."

With a groan, his mouth latched onto hers. His hands streaked over her body, stroking, kneading, cupping. Her body came alive beneath his hands. He pulled his mouth free.

Her breath came fast and hard as he nipped at her chin, her throat. He unzipped her dress, tossed the amethyst silk in a heap by her shoes. She yanked his shirt from his slacks, and while he dispensed with his shirt, she went to work on his belt and zipper.

He left her for a moment to kick away his pants and briefs, and to retrieve the packet from his pocket. And then he was beside her again. Clea shivered as his mouth closed over the tip of one breast while his hand slid down her stomach and tore away the strip of lace covering her. She gasped as his fingers entered her, and arched when he started to move.

Her nails cut into his shoulders as he increased the rhythm, until she felt herself quiver, then explode around his fingers. He brought her to climax after climax with his hands, with his mouth, with his tongue, until she wept with pleasure. And when she was sure she couldn't possibly experience anything so wondrous again, he thrust into her, filling her. Then he began to move with her until the music playing in her heart rose to a glass-shattering crescendo and sent them hurling together into the night sky. And as his arms tightened around her, and he found his release, she heard him whisper again, "I love you."

* * *

"I can't believe I'm doing this," Clea told him as she huddled beneath the sheets two nights later. "I've never canceled a business appointment in my life, and after all the trouble poor Gayle went to to get me reservations at that resort. What in the world will they think at the office when they find out I didn't even go?"

"They'll think you had something besides work on your mind for a change," he told her as he hung up the telephone and slipped into bed beside her. He eased his arm around her and pulled her close, enjoying the feel of her soft, naked skin pressed against his body. Already he could feel himself growing hard, wanting her again. He turned his face into her dark silken hair, breathed in that roses-and-rain scent that seemed such a part of her. Pushing aside her hair, he flicked the shell of her ear with his tongue.

She jerked to a sitting position, hauling the sheet up over her breasts. "I just thought of something. What do you think your family thought when they found out we canceled our reservation at the resort and checked into this bed-and-breakfast a stone's throw from their vineyard?"

Ryan shoved up onto his elbow. "They probably figured out that I couldn't make the hour drive to the resort because I had to make love with you. And guess what?" he said, tugging the sheet away to reveal her naked breasts. "They were right."

Color climbed up her cheeks, but her lips curved into a smile as he touched her. "We didn't even make it here that first night," she reminded him.

"I know. And you were incredible. Absolutely incredible."

"So were you," she told him.

"And I can just imagine what your brothers must be thinking when we didn't return to Chicago today like we were supposed to. What are you going to tell them?"

"That I haven't let you out of my sight." And he didn't intend to, either, Ryan promised himself. He eased a finger inside her, found her hot and wet. He rubbed the tender nub at her center. Her muscles tightened, convulsed around him. Sweat broke out across his brow at her trigger-quick response.

"Not by myself," she told him as he started to take her up again. "I want to feel you inside me, with me," she said, her hand racing down his chest to close around him.

Ryan groaned. He reached for the packet in the night-stand and nearly lost control when she insisted on helping him put it on. Then she was lowering herself onto him, filling herself with him, loving him. She moved slowly at first, a steady canter that he matched as she rode him. He gripped her hips, held her as the canter became a fast trot. And when he could wait no longer, Ryan pulled her beneath him and thrust himself into her—deep, deep, deeper—until he thought he must have joined their souls. He felt the quick flash and swore as the condom broke, but it was too late. They were already racing together down the furlong to the winner's ring.

"You okay?" he asked her when she emerged from the bathroom a short time later and joined him in bed. He pulled her into the circle of his arms.

"You mean other than the fact that my toes are permanently curled?" she teased.

"That good, huh?"

"Uh-hmm. But don't let it go to your head. Your ego doesn't need any boosting."

"Maybe not, but there is something I need."

"What?"

"To hear you say the words." Ryan turned her to face him, ran a finger down her cheek. "To hear you say that you love me."

"I love you," she whispered.

Relief flooded through him, and he folded her in his arms. "I was beginning to think you'd never say it," he told her. "I love you so much. I want to spend the rest of my life with you."

So caught up in joy, Ryan didn't notice her silence. "I have to confess something to you. Earlier when that condom broke, I was actually wishing you'd get pregnant so I could convince you we needed to get married."

"Couples don't 'have' to get married anymore just because the woman is pregnant," Clea told him.

"I know that. But you and I would. I realize we haven't talked about having kids or anything yet, but I know you love them as much as I do."

"Ryan—"

He ran his fingertips over her stomach, felt her quiver beneath his touch, and imagined his child growing inside her. "I intend to make lots of babies with you, Clea Mason. Who knows, you might even be pregnant right now."

Clea pushed his hand away and slipped out of the bed. She reached for her robe, wrapped it around her and turned away from him. "Trust me. I'm not pregnant."

"Maybe not yet," he told her, confused by her reaction.

"Not ever," she countered. "I'm sorry, Ryan. But I'm not going to have your babies and I'm not going to marry you. I never said that I would."

He felt as though he had been punched. He shot out of bed, grabbed her by the arm and turned her around to face him. "You want to explain what's going on here?"

She tipped up her chin, met his gaze. "It's quite simple. Marriage and children aren't in my plans."

Her words sliced right through his heart. He tightened his grip on her arm and stared at her. At the dark hair still tangled from his fingers, the delicate skin he'd marked with his whiskers, the mouth still pink and swollen from his kisses. "You expect me to believe that, after what we've shared? After you told me you loved me—gave yourself to me?"

"We had sex, Ryan, and I got caught up in the moment."

Ryan swore. "We made love. Love, dammit. And there's no way you're going to make me believe you could make love to me like that, tell me you love me, and not feel the same way I do."

Her eyes swam with tears, and she tried to pull away. "Please, Ryan. You have to let me go."

"Never," he told her, fear gripping his gut. "What is it? What's wrong?" he asked at the pained look on her face. "Please, Clea. Tell me. Whatever it is, we can work through it. We can fix it together."

She shook her head. "It can't be fixed. Not by you. Not by me. Not by anyone." Tears slid down her cheeks in big fat drops and nearly broke his heart in two. "I can't marry you, Ryan, because I love you too much."

"Duchess, I'm afraid that's not a very good reason for us not getting married," he joked, but his stomach churned at her serious expression.

"It's a very good reason. I love you too much to rob you of your chance to have what you want. What you deserve. A real wife. Children. A family."

"Clea, I—"

"You already know about my affair with Eric Ramsey six years ago," she began. "What your investigation didn't uncover was that I got pregnant as a result of that affair. I went to Eric to tell him about the baby, and that's when I found out he was still married. He told me that our affair had been fun, but he already had a wife and had no intention of divorcing her to marry me. He wrote down a name on a piece of paper, shoved it and some money in my hands, and told me if I was smart I'd get an abortion."

"The bastard!" Ryan's hands curled into fists. He wanted to make the other man pay for treating her so badly.

"I was hurt. And I felt so foolish and ashamed," she said swiping at her tears.

"You had nothing to be ashamed of," Ryan told her. He held her against him, aching for her. "You did what you felt you had to do."

She jerked away and stared up at his face. "I didn't have an abortion. I could never do that. I—I had a miscarriage. There were..." She swallowed. "There were complications, and now I can never..." Another sob shuddered through her. "I can never have children."

For a moment Ryan felt as though someone had pulled the rug out from under him. He'd always liked kids, assumed he'd have a mess of them. It had never occurred to him that he wouldn't. For one long heartbeat he felt cheated. Then he looked at Clea and knew it didn't matter—not as long as he had her.

"You think that matters to me?"

"Ryan, you aren't listening. I can never have *your* children."

"Clea, honey, I admit. I love kids. And yeah, I would like to have a house full. But I can live without kids. What I can't live without is you."

"And what about your family? Do you think it won't matter to them? They're counting on you to provide them with another generation of Fitzpatricks."

"That's my family's problem, not mine. Besides, I've got three brothers who can carry on the family name. Let them make a bunch of little Fitzpatricks."

"You think it won't matter to you now, but what about later? Can you honestly say that you won't mind missing that special joy of knowing you helped to create a life? That you won't miss watching that life you helped to create, that life that's a part of you, grow up and create new lives, new children, all parts of you?"

"You're talking progeny here, Clea. The basic continuation of the human race. I don't think there's any chance of mankind becoming extinct because I fail to add my sperm to the cause. Besides there are a lot of kids in the world without parents. We can adopt. Believe me, the fact that my sperm didn't create him or her isn't going to make the child any less mine." He reached out to her, framed her face with his hands. "But either way, whether we adopt or not, I'm fine with it. As long as I have you. *You're* what matters to me. You're the only one I need. The rest, we'll work out."

"What if you're wrong? What if someday you grow to hate me for cheating you of a family? What then?"

Ryan shook his head, searched for the words to convince her. "That's never going to happen. I love you. Nothing's ever going to change that."

"I know you believe that. But sometimes love just isn't enough."

"I'm willing to take a chance that ours is," he told her, laying his heart and soul at her feet. "Trust me, Clea. Trust in us, in our love for each other. Marry me."

"I can't. I just can't take that big of a risk."

Her words ripped through him like a bullet. "So where does that leave us?"

"We could still be lovers."

"That's not enough for me."

"I can't offer you anything else."

The pain inside him threatened to bring him to his knees. Sheer pride kept him on his feet. "Then I guess there's no point in hanging around here for those two extra days."

"I guess not. We should probably just go."

"Whatever you say." Anger and hurt attacked him from both sides, delivering painful jabs to his midsection. He snatched up the phone, requested his car be brought around and their airline tickets changed for the next available flight to Chicago.

After slamming down the phone, he retrieved Clea's suitcase and tossed it on top of the bed. "We're on standby for a flight that leaves in three hours," he told her. "When we get back, I'm going to find the sicko who's been threatening you and wrap up this case. And then I'm getting out of your life for good.''

And maybe then, Ryan told himself as he stormed into the bathroom and shoved the door closed, the prospect of living his life without her wouldn't hurt nearly so much.

Ten

The letter was waiting for her. Fear crawled along Clea's skin as she recognized the frighteningly familiar handwriting on an envelope once again propped up in front of the vase of flowers. Panic threatened to override the exhaustion of enduring Ryan's icy silence and a night spent in an airport waiting on a series of standby flights. Willing herself to remain calm, she set down her purse and keys.

"Son of a—" Ryan bit off the rest. "I'd like to know how in the hell he managed to get past the alarm system and my guy downstairs to leave this in here." Dumping their suitcases on the floor, he marched over to the table. She expected him to whip out his handkerchief and carefully open the letter as she had watched him do several times in the past. Instead he grabbed the envelope and ripped it open. Scowling, he scanned the two pages.

She used the moment to study him, to drink in the sight of him while she still could. He looked as tired and miserable as she felt, Clea decided, noting the dark whiskers shadowing his lean cheeks and jaw, the tired lines from lack of sleep, the angry frown pinching his lips.

He glanced up, black fury in his eyes, and crumbled the letter in his fist. Another first, Clea realized and she was sure his lack of care with the letter was an indication of how deep his anger ran. She had caught a glimpse of that anger and that brief flicker of doubt when she'd told him she would never be able to give him a child.

"I'll be back in a few minutes," he said and started to storm past her.

"Ryan, wait." She touched his arm, and he immediately froze. His glacial expression stung, just as his silence had stung during the long night spent waiting at the airport and during the flight from San Francisco this morning. She dropped her hand. "What does it say?" she asked him, fearing the answer, but knowing she couldn't hide from it any longer. She hadn't wanted to know what had been in the last few letters. She had been satisfied to let Ryan shield her from the contents. But soon Ryan would be gone, and she couldn't go on hiding, trying to pretend the nightmare wasn't real.

"The usual stuff."

"Maybe I should read it," she said, and reached for the letter in his fist.

"No!"

His answer was swift and harsh and sent an icy chill through her. "Why not?" She searched his guarded expression. "What is it that you aren't telling me?"

"He was in Napa Valley."

Her heart stopped a moment. Suddenly her knees felt shaky, but she willed herself not to fall apart. "I want to see the letter, Ryan."

"I already told you what you need to know. He was in Napa Valley. There's no reason to put yourself through anything more by reading the thing. It'll only upset you."

"Then, I'll just have to be upset. Give me the letter," she ordered, holding out her hand.

"Fine. Go ahead and read the damn thing, then." He shoved the crumpled sheets into her palm.

Annoyed by the slight tremor in her fingers, Clea smoothed out the sheet of ivory stationery and stared at the longhand that had caused her so much grief during the past several months. She could feel the color drain from her face, the bile rise in her throat, but she forced herself to finish reading. Then she handed it back to him.

Ryan swore. He took her by the arm and led her over to the couch. "Sit down," he commanded and shoved her head down between her knees. When the dizziness passed and she lifted her head, he handed her a snifter of brandy. "Drink this."

"It's barely past noon. I don't want a—"

"Dammit, Clea. Drink it, or I'll pour it down your throat."

For a moment she considered arguing, but decided against it. She took a sip. The brandy slid down her throat like liquid fire, making her cough. She shoved the glass at him. "That's it," she said, her voice hoarse but her nerves steadier. "I'm not drinking any more."

"It's enough. At least you've got some color coming back into your cheeks."

"I'm okay now," she said, but picked up the pillow on the couch, needing something to hold on to, wishing it could be him. "I thought I'd escaped for a little while. But I hadn't. He knew what I wore to your cousins' party. He was there watching me the whole time."

"Yeah, I know. I should have listened to you when you said you had a feeling someone was watching you. If I hadn't been so wrapped up in spinning pipe dreams about us, I might have been able to catch him."

"It's not your fault. You weren't the only one caught up in those dreams that night. So was I."

"Just not enough to take a chance on them," he said, his voice bitter. "Wait here while I check out the place. I suspect everything's clean just like last time, but I want to be sure."

Clea closed her eyes and listened to the sound of Ryan moving from room to room. And she ached. For him. For herself. For what they could never have. Not even the sick letter or the knowledge that a madman had gotten past the guard and alarm system could override the pain inside her. She had thought she had known heartache before, that she had known loss. But nothing had prepared her for this agonizing emptiness that giving up Ryan had left inside her.

"The place is clean. No sign of forced entry. Are you sure no one has a key to this place but you?"

Clea opened her eyes, and she ached all over again just looking at him. "You're the only other person I've given one to."

"What about a spare? Don't you keep one somewhere in case you have an emergency or get locked out?"

"I have one at the office. I keep it locked in my desk drawer."

"And who else has a key to your desk besides you?"

"No one," Clea told him, then paused.

"What?"

"A key to all of the desks and files are kept in a key lockbox at Destinations. They're coded and tagged for reference in case there's an emergency and access is needed."

"Who has a key to the lockbox?" Ryan asked.

"As office manager, I do. And since they're the owners, Maggie and James each have a key." Her gaze flew to his face, knowing where he was headed and disliking it.

"And my uncle James was in Napa Valley when you were there—and looking very unhappy, too."

Clea shot to her feet. "He was lonely for Maggie and disappointed that your aunt wasn't able to come with him."

"He didn't look very disappointed when he was chatting with you at the party."

"Ryan, don't," she warned, wishing she could tell him the truth. That his uncle's talks with her were cries for advice and help because he feared his wife had fallen out of love with him. But Clea had sworn to keep his secret.

"What was it that was so important that he found it necessary to track you down at the inn to talk about? And what business problem compelled him to call you three times in the past two days here when he couldn't reach you again at the inn?"

Clea blinked. "James called me here?"

"It's on your caller ID box."

She hiked up her chin. "I appreciate your thoroughness," she told him. "But you're wrong about James. And I refuse to stand here and listen to any more of your insinuations about him. He isn't the one sending me the letters or calling me. He wouldn't do that."

"How do you know? I told you he had an addiction years ago. That he—"

"I told you, I don't want to hear this."

She started to move past him, but Ryan blocked her path. Fury turned his blue eyes nearly black. Anger shimmered from him like the heat of a desert sun. "This blind loyalty you seem to have for my uncle is touching, but foolish. Whether you want to accept it or not, his attitude toward you is obsessive. This…" He held up the letter in his fist. "This is the raving of a man who's obsessed with you. And the person who wrote this isn't going to stop until he has you."

"Then do what I'm paying you to do. Stop him," she snapped, exhaustion and heartache pushing her to the edge.

Ryan's jaw clenched. "I intend to, Duchess. But not because it's my job. The job doesn't have a thing to do with it. I'm going to stop him because I love you, dammit. Do you have any idea what it would do to me if something happened to you?''

Then he took her mouth in a savage kiss. A kiss that spoke of hunger, of love, of frustration, and soothed all those aching, lonely places in her heart. When he released her mouth, he practically snarled, ''I love you. And I'll be damned if I'm going to let you go.''

She didn't want to be let go, and she didn't want to let him go either. She remembered that split second of doubt she'd seen in his eyes when she'd told him life with her would mean no children. Nothing had changed. She still was incapable of being a true wife to him. She couldn't risk marrying him only to have him grow to hate her.

As though sensing her resistance, he said, ''Can we at least agree to discuss this stupid idea of yours about the importance of reproduction later?''

She nodded.

''I have to go out for a couple of hours. Will you be okay by yourself?''

''I'll be fine. I was going to rest awhile and then go into the office later this afternoon.''

''All right.'' He brushed his mouth across hers. ''Jake's on watch outside, and I should be back in a little while to take you to the office. If I'm not, I want you to wait here for me. Understand?''

''I understand.''

Damn, Ryan thought, smacking his fist against his office door. He'd hit another dead end, and his gut told him time was running out. He'd checked the airline passenger lists in search of another name besides his uncle's who had been in San Francisco the same time as Clea. He had thought he'd hit pay dirt when he'd seen Ramsey's name on a flight out the day before Clea's, and a reservation for him at one of the plush resorts in the Valley. But the man had been researching properties for the Don Levy account and apparently trying out the beds with his much-younger secretary. Ryan scratched his name from the list.

That left him with three suspects. The fresh-out-of-school Philip whom Clea had hired six months ago and who had a monster-size crush on her. Working for a travel agency, it was possible the kid had booked a flight under another name and flown out to California without his name showing up on any passenger list.

Larry. He circled the name of the computer whiz who had sold the agency's computer system to Clea, and set it up. He'd been attracted enough to Clea to ask her out before Clea had steered him to her smitten assistant. It wouldn't be the first time a man married one woman, but lusted for another. And the guy's wife worked for a travel agency, and he knew his way around computers. He underlined Larry's name and the flights to and from Vegas. Vegas wasn't that far away. He could hop a commuter flight or rent a car. Except that Gayle had mentioned Larry was working on a big system at one of the casinos, and the reservation at the hotel checked out. Ryan made a note to talk with the head of the computer department to be sure.

He stared at the final name on his list—James Donatelli. Uncle James. Ryan tossed down his pencil and pinched the area above the bridge of his nose as he considered the evidence against the man. His uncle had been in Napa Valley when Clea was there. He'd been without his wife. He'd been upset and almost desperate in his need to speak to Clea—so much so that he had tracked them down at the inn. Everything pointed to his uncle. He didn't want it to be his uncle. What would it do to his aunt, his family?

"Hey, little brother." Sean tapped on his door and stuck his head inside. "Clea let you off your leash for a few hours?"

Ryan barked at him. "Don't you have something better to do than pester me?"

"Nope. Just wrapped up my last case. Mike's meeting

me at Joe's for a sandwich and a couple of beers. Want to come?''

''Can't. I'm supposed to pick up Clea and take her into the office.''

''This late?'' Sean asked, scrounging in his desk drawer until he found the stash of chocolate-nut bars.

''What time is it anyway?'' Ryan asked, suddenly realizing he'd been going at it for a lot longer than he'd planned.

''Almost five o'clock.''

''Damn.'' Ryan grabbed the phone and punched in Clea's number. When he got her machine, his palms began to sweat. He hung up and beeped Jake Delaney.

''What's wrong?'' Sean asked as he sat down across from Ryan and propped his feet up on the desk.

''Clea doesn't answer.'' The phone rang and he grabbed it. ''Fitzpatrick.''

''It's Delaney.''

''I'm not getting an answer at Clea's apartment. Do you know if she's all right?''

''Seemed fine to me when she left.''

His heart rate slowed a notch. ''She left? How long ago?''

His rapid-fire questions apparently didn't faze Delaney, because the man answered in the same steady drawl that marked him as a Southerner. ''Left here about an hour and a half ago with her assistant. Pretty blonde named Gayle. Said to tell you she'd be at the office.''

''Thanks.'' Ryan slapped down the receiver. ''I'm going to kill that woman.''

Sean threw back his head and laughed. ''Look at you. The woman's got you jumping through hoops already, and you two aren't even married yet. Can't wait to see what happens when she puts that ring through your nose.''

Ryan shoved his brother's feet off his desk. ''You know, bro, I'm going to take real pleasure in watching you eat those words when some sweet, little thing comes along and ties you up in knots.''

''Ain't going to happen to me,'' Sean assured him. ''Too many women for me to settle down with just one.''

''Right,'' Ryan told him as he yanked open the door to leave. ''That's what I used to think, too.''

''Honestly, Ryan. I don't know why you're so upset,'' Clea told him as he scowled at her from across her desk.

''Do the words 'wait for me' sound familiar?''

''I've already explained to you that the main computer system went on the fritz this afternoon, and Gayle called me because she couldn't reach Maggie or James. Larry's already on his way out to fix the thing, but someone has to be here to let him in and lock up after he's finished.''

Ryan flattened his palms on her desk and leaned in, crowding her space. ''Then let Gayle wait for Larry. He's *her* husband.''

Clea sighed and strove for patience. ''She would have, but tonight's her biology class at the university, and she couldn't miss it because she has an exam.''

''Then get someone else to come wait for Larry. You and I need to talk, Clea. About my uncle James.''

The private line on her desk rang, and Clea reached for the receiver. ''Clea Mason.''

''I was beginning to think you'd never come back.'' Her hand trembled at the sound of that raspy whisper.

''You looked so beautiful dancing in the moonlight. I pretended it was me who was holding you, making love to you, instead of him.''

Something in her face must have clued Ryan because he was beside her in a flash, yanking open and digging in the desk drawers, dumping out papers and supplies. His fingers chased along the length of a wire cord. He snagged a little white box from beneath a stack of business cards. Then she remembered—the caller ID box he had insisted on install-ing, along with the tap.

Ryan stared at the box's ID. Pain washed over his face a moment and was replaced by a cold, dark anger that made her shiver. She knew he had suspected his uncle, and she was so sure he'd been wrong. This couldn't be James. It couldn't be.

"The waiting's almost over," the voice continued on the phone. "Soon, you're going to be mine, Clea. When you are, I'm going to—"

"No," she cried, her stomach pitching as she recalled the things he had said he was going to do to her.

Ryan snatched the phone from her hand. "The game's up, Uncle James. I know—"

The line went dead.

"No," she told him, pushing away from the desk to stand. "That wasn't James. It couldn't be him."

"It *was* him, Clea. That's his name and number on the caller ID box."

"Then the box is wrong. It's a mistake. It has to be. James would never do something like this to me."

Ryan caught her by the shoulders and turned her to face the desk. Snagging the white box from the heap in the drawer, he forced her to look at it again. "Read it, Clea. James Donatelli," he read the name flashing with the phone number. "There's no mistake. It was him. I'm sorry. I know how much you care about him. And dammit, so do I." He pitched the box back into the desk drawer. "The man's my uncle. I've loved him most of my life. Don't you think I wish it wasn't true?"

"It isn't. I don't care what that thing says," she coun-tered, jabbing her finger at the box. "I'm telling you there's been a mistake. There has to be another explanation."

"Then let's go find out what it is." He grabbed the red jacket of her suit from the coatrack and handed it to her. "We're going over to his house."

"No." Clea dug in her heels. "I'm not going to accuse a man I care about, a man I admire, of something I know isn't true."

"Fine. Then I'll go by myself after I drop you off at your apartment."

"But I can't leave now. I told you I have to wait for Larry to come fix the computer." And as though on cue, she heard the tap against the glass door out front. "That must be him now."

"Tell him to come back in the morning."

"I can't. That's what I tried to tell you earlier," she said, taking her keys from her desk drawer and heading for the outer office. "The machine has to be fixed tonight. We have to run tickets in the morning for two big cruise groups." And if she concentrated on work she wouldn't have time to dwell on that phone call and who was behind it. Or her feelings for Ryan. Punching in the deactivate code for the alarm, she unlocked the door.

"Hi. Sorry I'm so late. Got here as soon as I could."

"Thanks, Larry. But I'm the one who should be apologizing for making you give up your evening like this. I really do appreciate it."

"Any time," he said, giving her a warm smile.

"Hello, Granger."

"Ryan," Larry said, taking the hand extended to him.

Clea couldn't help but notice the differences between the two men. Ryan with his dark hair and easy charm towered over Larry by at least six inches and had to outweigh the smaller man by at least forty pounds. With his thinning hair pulled back into a short ponytail and his quiet manner, Larry Granger fit the stereotypical image of the computer nerd.

Larry turned his attention back to her. "Gayle said the machine started spitting out tickets by the armload, and then it froze up altogether."

"Yes. We tried a number of things, but it just seems to have died now."

"Don't worry. I'll get her fixed for you. I'd never let you down, Clea." He walked over to the main terminal, set down his tool kit and opened it up. "Let me take a look at this little beauty here and see if I can find out just what her problem is."

"You're a lifesaver, Larry," she told him. "I know Gayle thinks she's the lucky one because she married you, but I think Destinations is lucky. I swear, I don't know what we'd do around here without you."

"I think it's the other way around," Larry told her. "I'm the one who's lucky. Finding Destinations made all my dreams come true."

"From what I hear, we're just small stuff now that your business is expanding."

"That's not true. I could have ten companies, but you'll always be special to me," he told her as he loosened the screws at the back of the computer's frame.

"I'm sure the fact that you met Gayle here has a little something to do with it," she teased him.

"Can't say I blame him," Ryan said, putting an arm around Clea. He stared into her eyes. "I'm pretty fond of this place myself since it's where I met you."

"Heard you just got back from the Donatelli Vineyards," Larry cut in, surprising her since he didn't often make conversation. "Did you have a good time?"

"Yes, we did," Clea replied.

"Must have been nice sampling all those wines," he said, going to work with the small screwdriver on the next set of screws at the computer's front.

"It was. But it's probably a good thing I don't live there. I'm afraid I could get used to having my own wine cellar to select from all too easily."

Larry lifted the top off the computer and unveiled a puzzle of silver and copper metal components and memory chips. "But you'd choose the '95 cabernet sauvignon. The prizewinning one."

"Why, yes. That's right," Clea admitted, surprised at his mention of the wine she'd favored during her evening with the Donatellis. "How did you know that?"

"Mr. Donatelli must have mentioned it." Larry looked down at the maze of computer parts he called a motherboard. "I'm afraid this might take a while."

"How long?" Ryan asked.

Larry rubbed his jaw. "Hard to say. My guess is there's a short circuit in one of the ports." He pointed to the prongs that covered the board, lined up like a platoon of soldiers. "I'm going to have to test each of them until I find out which one's the problem."

"Any idea how long that'll take?" Ryan repeated.

"Can't say. I might hit the bad one right off, or it could take me a couple of hours. You want me to hold off and come back tomorrow?"

"No," Clea answered. "We have to be ready to print tickets and itineraries in the morning. Please, Larry, go ahead and start working on it. I'll be in my office working on my portable if you need me for anything."

Ryan took her cue and followed her back to her office. He shut the door and started toward her. "Before you say a word," she warned, "please don't mention anything about your suspicions of James while Larry's here. Sometimes walls talk. And I'd hate for anything like that to be overheard or misconstrued."

"All right," Ryan agreed. "But when Larry's finished, I'm taking you home and going over to my uncle's house for some answers. Then when this mess is behind us, you and I are going to sit down and have a serious talk."

"Ryan, don't—"

He touched her cheek, and she could feel her resistance start to melt. "Later. When this is over we'll talk. But make no mistake, I meant what I said earlier. I'm not letting you go."

"All right. We'll talk. Later."

The phone rang again and Clea stiffened. Ryan grabbed it and barked out, "Hello." The line went dead, but once again his uncle's name and number flashed on the box.

"I'm going over there," Ryan told her as he shoved the receiver down on the phone. "Come on, Clea."

"No!"

A tap sounded at the door and Larry stuck his head inside. "Sorry to interrupt." His gaze swiveled between them. "I'm going to have to run back to my shop to get a part."

"How long is that going to take?" Ryan asked him.

"About twenty minutes to go to my shop and get back. After that, maybe another forty minutes to an hour on the machine."

"That's fine, Larry. You go on ahead," Clea told him.

But twenty-five minutes later, Larry still hadn't returned and she still refused to leave. Ryan paced the length of Clea's office and glanced at his watch for what had to be the tenth time in as many minutes. Clea hit the save key on her laptop. "Ryan, for pity's sake. Why don't you just go see James and get it over with."

"I'm not leaving you here alone," he told her. "Let me see if I can get ahold of Sean or Michael."

By the time he had hung up a third time and muttered something about *fools* and *worthless brothers,* Clea had no trouble surmising he hadn't reached them. "No luck, huh?"

"No," Ryan admitted. "The idiots either don't have their beepers with them or they were having too good a time at Joe's Place to call me."

Based on the Fitzpatrick brothers' reputation and the way women flocked to them, she suspected it wasn't Joe keeping either of the men occupied. Not unless Joe was short for Josephine or Jo Anne.

"Let me try the office again."

Clea stayed his hand as he reached for the phone again. "Ryan, please just go I—I need some space. Some time to think."

"I'm not leaving you alone," he repeated.

I'm not going to be alone for very long. Larry's due back any minute now. And I mean it. I need some space. If you're right and it's James calling me, I'll be okay."

He hesitated.

"I'll be fine," she assured him and urged him to the outer office entrance.

"All right. I'll go. But I want you to lock the door behind me and set the alarm."

"I will."

He captured her face in his hands and kissed her slowly, tenderly, until her head started to spin with the taste of him. "I love you," he whispered as he released her. "I'll be back as soon as I can."

Her lips still warm from Ryan's kiss, her thoughts still filled with him, she somehow managed to lock the door and reactivate the alarm. She pressed her fingers against the glass to where his fingers were splayed on the opposite side, mating their palms through the glass. He mouthed the words, "I love you" again, and her heart swelled.

And then he was running to his car, backing it out of the lot and driving away. She watched him until the red taillights disappeared, before turning and starting back toward her office. She had taken no more than two steps when she stopped in her tracks.

Spinning around, she went back to the door. She cupped her hands around her face and against the glass, and peered out into the darkness, searching for the eyes that she was sure were out there watching.

Eleven

"**R**yan, my boy, what a surprise. Come in," James Donatelli said, opening the door to welcome him. "Is Clea with you?"

"She's at Destinations."

"At this time of the evening?" James asked as they entered the living room. "I thought now that you two were engaged, the girl would stop spending so much time at that office."

"There was a problem with the computer, and she had to wait on the repair guy to come back with a part."

"Larry Granger, I take it."

"Yes," Ryan said, noting his uncle's almost jubilant mood as he walked over to the bar. The elegant dark suit and patterned tie, the thick silver hair combed straight back from his face, were all the same, but there was a briskness in his step, a glint in his eyes that hadn't been there the last time Ryan had seen him.

"Granger's a good man. He'll find the problem in no time and correct it." He lifted a shot glass. "Drink?"

"No, thanks," Ryan said, surprised to see the man pour himself a ginger ale. He would have bet that his uncle's obsession with Clea would also have triggered the man's earlier addiction to alcohol.

"Sit down, son."

Too edgy to sit, Ryan said, "I'd rather stand."

His uncle took a sip of his drink. "Just as well, I guess. I only have a few minutes to give you anyway. I've got very special plans for this evening."

Anger gnawed at his gut when he saw the expression on his uncle's face, and Ryan wondered if those plans included the man's sick fantasies for Clea. "This won't take long," he told him. Because tonight, he thought to himself, it will all come to an end. It might tear my family apart, but it can't be helped. Clea will be safe.

"So what brings you here?"

"The phone call you made to Clea this evening."

His uncle frowned. "I didn't call Clea this evening."

"No?"

"No," his uncle said, eyeing him strangely. "I haven't spoken to her since I called her at the inn in Napa Valley three days ago. I left a couple of messages on her machine, but I haven't heard back from her yet. That's one of the reasons I was so surprised to see you here. I didn't realize the two of you had gotten back from California yet. I'd heard you'd extended your visit."

"We had a change of plans and got back earlier today. But then, you already knew that, didn't you. You found that out when Clea answered your call tonight on her private line at the office."

James's silver brows pulled together. "Ryan, I already told you, I haven't spoken with Clea since she got back."

"No, you didn't actually speak with her, did you? You just whispered your filth to her over the phone."

James smacked his glass down on the table, sloshing ginger ale over the sides and onto the polished mahogany. "Just what in the hell are you implying, boy?"

"I'm not implying anything. I'm telling you that I know it's you who's been calling Clea. And my guess is it's you who's been sending her the letters, and that it was you who grabbed her at the theater, too."

"You're out of your mind. The girl's like a daughter to me. Your aunt and I are the ones who had her hire you in the first place."

"Cut the crap, Uncle James. You screwed up this time. You knew Clea had refused to have a tap put on her office phone, so you didn't bother scrambling the phone numbers or using a pay phone when you called her at the office tonight. But what you didn't know was that I convinced her to let me install a caller ID box on her line. And when you called her tonight, it was your name and your number that showed up on that little box."

"I don't give a damn what any box says. I'm telling you, I didn't call Clea. How could you even think I'd do such a thing to her?"

"Maybe I can think it because I know you're in love with her, dammit."

"In love with her?" his uncle repeated, looking at him as though *he* were the one who'd lost his mind. "Let me tell you something, son. Clea's my business associate, and she's one of the best friends I've ever had, and yes, you're right, I do love her. But not in the way that you mean. There's only one woman I'm in love with that way, and she's my wife."

Damn, but the man sounded so sincere. And there was a part of Ryan who wanted to believe him. He thought once again of that special uncle, the man he had loved most of his life. Remembering Clea's ghost-white face tonight when that call had come through, however, he shoved the sentiment aside. "But your wife hasn't been around much lately. Has she, Uncle James?"

James bunched his hands into fists. "I didn't realize you were keeping such close tabs on your aunt's and my activities."

"Close enough to notice that you haven't been very happy for quite some time, and close enough to notice that the woman you seem to always turn to is Clea. You want to tell me what was so all-fired important that you called her three times at home during the past two days?"

A flush crawled up his uncle's neck, staining his skin a deep red. "That's none of your business."

"I'm making it my business. I'm not going to let you hurt Clea."

Shock registered on his uncle's face.

"I'd never do anything to hurt her. I told you, I love her like a daughter."

"The same way you loved booze, Uncle James?"

His uncle flinched as though he had been punched. "That's low of you, Ryan. Really low."

And it was, Ryan admitted to himself, recalling his aunt and uncle's separation years before. His uncle had hit rock bottom when he had entered that rehabilitation program. But when he came out, he had been a changed man and had won back his wife. Ryan had thought James's problems had been licked.

Until now.

"Whether you believe me or not, I've kept my promise to your aunt. I haven't touched a drink since she and I reconciled ten years ago."

Ryan searched his uncle's face. "Then how do you explain your name and number on that caller ID box? And why all the urgent phone calls and private conferences with Clea?"

"I can't explain the caller ID box, but I swear to you I didn't place any calls. As for my relationship with Clea, well you were right about my not being happy." His uncle began to pace. "I was worried I was losing your aunt, that she didn't love me anymore. She was so wrapped up in this new business venture of hers and there didn't seem to be any room in her life for me. I went to Clea for advice. To ask her to help me win back my wife."

But Clea had never told Ryan. She'd been a good friend and had kept his uncle's secret. "But what did you think Clea could do?"

"I wasn't sure. I only knew that she and Maggie were close. That Maggie respected her. I wanted her to intervene, to talk to Maggie for me."

"Did she?"

"No." A wistful smile curved his mouth. "Said I had to do that myself. She suggested I tell Maggie how I was feeling. But I was afraid to. I was worried your aunt would think it was like before, when I became so possessive of her. I was afraid this time I'd lose her for good. I love her so much. I didn't know what I'd do if I lost her."

He knew just what the man meant, because it was exactly the way he felt about Clea.

"But I'm not going to lose her."

His uncle's face brightened. A smile of satisfaction spread across his lips. "When I couldn't reach Clea, I flew out to New York where your aunt was. I told the hotel to hold all her calls and tossed those marketing people out of her suite, then I laid my feelings on the line for her. Told her I love her, didn't want to live without her, but wanted my wife back—and that I wasn't leaving until I got her."

Ryan grinned. "I take it you got her."

"You bet, I did. She and I are going out for dinner and dancing tonight. Then we're coming back here and christening that new hot tub we've never used. I've given the housekeeper the rest of the week off and told the office not to expect to see either of us until next week."

"Congratulations," Ryan said, relief flooding through

him. He extended his hand. "I'm sorry about the accusations. I didn't want to believe it could be you, but I couldn't let anything happen to Clea. Nothing means more to me than she does."

"I know, son. I know. I just wish I had an explanation as to why my name and number showed up on that box tonight."

"Me, too," Ryan said, disturbed now that he knew his uncle was innocent. That meant the real culprit was still out there and Clea was alone, with only the innocuous Larry for protection. "I'm going to make some calls in the morning, talk to an electronics expert and see if he can tell me how this guy did the number switch so that your name showed up."

James walked Ryan to the door. "You don't have to wait until morning. Why don't you just ask Larry Granger. I bet he could tell you."

"Granger? He's a computer whiz, Uncle James. I'm talking electronic equipment here. I think this involves a little more than memory chips and discs."

"So, ask Granger. The kid's got an undergraduate degree in electrical engineering. Before he got into computers, he used to work at NASA doing some electrical design stuff for the space program. Gave it up because he didn't like having to deal with people all the time."

Ryan's heart seemed to freeze in his chest. "You sure about that? Him having an electronics background?"

"Of course, I'm sure. And he's good. Why just this past week I was having a reception problem with the phone and television in my study. I had Gayle call around, but she couldn't get anyone out for a week. Well, she told Larry about it, and the fellow showed up here at my door the next evening, and lickety-split, the problem's fixed. Both the TV set and phone are working like a charm now. And the kid wouldn't even let me pay him. Insisted all he wanted was a bottle of the Donatelli cabernet sauvignon as his fee."

Ryan frowned. "I didn't realize Granger was a wine connoisseur."

"Surprised me, too. He said Clea mentioned how much she had enjoyed it, and said he wanted to try it."

Uneasiness creeping up on him, Ryan replayed the earlier conversation between Granger and Clea in his head. "I thought *you* were the one who told him about the wine."

"Me? I haven't seen Larry since last week. After I came back from California, I flew out to New York to get Maggie. We didn't get back until last night."

Stark fear swept through Ryan. "Jesus! It's him! Larry's the one after Clea, and he's alone with her now!"

"Oh, my God!"

Ryan raced out to his car, his uncle chasing behind him. "Call the police and tell them to get over to Destinations," he commanded. Shifting into reverse, he sent the car flying down the driveway. Tires squealing, he floored the accelerator. He punched in the number at Clea's office, and the phone started to ring.

Answer. Answer.

But the phone continued to ring. Cutting the connection, he hit the auto-dial number for his brother. Sean picked up on the second ring.

"Fitzpatrick's Haven for Single Females."

"Sean, it's Ryan. Find Mike and get over to Destinations now! Larry Granger's the one behind the letters and calls. And he's got Clea."

Clea raced back to her office to catch the ringing phone. "Hello," she answered a little breathless, only to hear the dial tone. "Great," she muttered as she hung up and sat down behind her desk.

Restless, she rubbed her hands up and down her arms, unable to shake the uneasy feeling she'd had since Ryan had left. She was probably just overreacting, she told herself. It would be amazing if she weren't on emotional overload. The phone calls and letters had been scaring her silly for months, but they had brought her Ryan. After years of leading such a quiet, orderly life, Ryan Fitzpatrick had managed to turn her world and her heart upside down. And despite his foolish suspicions about James, she did love him. And for whatever crazy reason, Ryan loved her, too. Maybe he was telling her the truth. Maybe her inability to have babies wouldn't matter. He'd said they could adopt.

Dragging her thoughts back to the present, she looked at the stack of customer folders in front of her, waiting to be ticketed in the morning. What in the devil had happened to Larry? she wondered. She hesitated a moment and picked up the phone.

"Hello," came a hoarse-sounding reply.

"Gayle? Gayle, is that you?"

"Clea," her assistant repeated her name, sobbing.

"Gayle, honey, are you okay?"

"Yes."

But Clea didn't think so. Gayle sounded as though she were crying. "I was calling to see if Larry was there. He left here about thirty minutes ago to get a part for the computer, but he isn't back yet."

"He's not here. He...he left a few minutes ago."

"Good. Then I'm sure he'll be here soon. How did you do on your biology exam?"

"Fine," she replied, barely more than a whisper.

"Gayle, are you sure you're all right?"

"I'm just not feeling very well. Clea, I—"

"Yes?"

"Good night."

The dial tone buzzed in her ear. Clea looked at the phone a moment, surprised and concerned by Gayle's reaction. Then she remembered the other woman complaining that her husband was working so much. And here I am, she thought, making the poor man work tonight. Promising herself she would make it up to Gayle, Clea grabbed the top file on the stack and went back to work.

Deep in the task of punching in flight data, Clea jumped at the tapping sound at the front door. "At last," she said, grabbing the keys and hurrying toward the door, anxious to see Ryan.

Larry waved to her. Swallowing her disappointment, she unlocked the door and deactivated the code. "Gee, that's a mighty big part," she said, noting the large canvas tote bag in his hand.

"Just a few things I'll need to finish the job," he explained with a smile that made his dark eyes gleam. "Gayle said you called for me."

"Yes, I was just wondering if there was a problem. You were gone so long," she replied, relocking the door and setting the alarm again. Clea frowned. "But Gayle told me you'd already left the house."

"I had," he said smoothly. "She called me on my cell phone." He headed for the main computer terminal, his step more energetic, almost nervous. "Ryan not back yet?"

"No, but he should be here soon." She started to mention Gayle's illness, but decided against it. "I'll be working in my office. Let me know when you're ready to go, and I'll let you out."

"Will do," Larry said, looking up from the computer board and smiling. "I shouldn't be too much longer."

Clea paused, turned back and looked at Larry. His head was bent over the computer, his fingers playing along the complex board like a violinist's on a Stradivarius. A smile snaked across his lips, making her uneasy. She shook her head. Telling herself she was imagining things, she headed for her office.

Minutes later, seated at her desk, Clea rubbed at her temples and then froze, struck again by that strange sensation of being watched. Her gaze shot to the doorway. "Larry, for heaven's sake. You scared me," she told him, pressing a hand to her still fast-beating heart. "Are you finished?" she asked, glancing at the canvas bag in his hand.

"Not quite." Stepping into the office, he closed the door and locked it.

Her stomach fell. "Then maybe you should just forget about fixing the computer tonight. The tickets can wait another day," she said, nerves taut. "It's really getting late, and I know Gayle isn't feeling well. You should go home now. You can come back tomorrow and finish."

"I can't wait until tomorrow. I've already waited too long for you," he whispered.

Clea's blood turned to ice in her veins. Fear crawled along her skin at the sound of that voice. "You need to go home to Gayle, Larry," she said, curling her fingers around the arms of her chair. "Gayle needs you. She's not feeling well."

"I had to hurt her. I didn't want to, but I had to," he said. Opening the canvas bag, he removed two wineglasses and a bottle of '95 cabernet sauvignon from Donatelli Vineyards.

"W-what did you do to Gayle, Larry? How badly is she hurt?"

He opened the wine and poured out two glasses. "She found out about us, you know. When I went home to get the wine, she was there, digging in my things. She found a letter I'd written to you. She was very upset. She didn't understand that we love one another. She threatened to call Fitzpatrick, to have him try to stop us from meeting tonight."

Clea swallowed, fighting back the panic choking her. "Larry, tell me what's wrong with Gayle."

"She had a headache, so I gave her something to make her sleep." He offered Clea a glass of the wine. "Take it," he insisted in that menacing whisper. "It's your favorite. I got it especially for you."

"Larry, I'm worried about Gayle," she said, her hand

trembling as she took the glass from him. "I think we should go check on her."

Anger snapped in his eyes. "I told you she's asleep. And I don't want to talk about her. I only married her in the first place to please you. You seemed to want me to like her so much. But it was a mistake. She never understood that it wasn't her that I loved. It was you." He moved closer, ran his fingers down her cheek. Clea shuddered. "I've always loved you. Let's toast. To us."

He tapped his glass against hers and took a drink. "Why aren't you drinking?" he snapped.

Clea lifted the glass to her lips, sure she would gag if she tried to swallow. *Ryan. Oh, Ryan. Where are you?*

"Don't you like it? It's your favorite."

"Yes," she lied and forced herself to take another sip.

"You're so beautiful," he said, touching her face. She cringed at his touch, but he didn't seem to notice. "I watched you on the veranda at that party. You looked like an angel dancing. I wanted to dance with you. I almost came to you that night." Clea squeezed her eyes shut at the realization that he had been there watching her. "Come," he said taking the glass from her and setting it on the desk. "Dance with me now."

"There's no music," she told him, shuddering as he took her hand and led her from behind the desk.

"Yes, there is. Don't you hear it? It's our song."

"Our song?" Clea repeated, her body stiff as he led her into a waltz.

"The one they were playing the night we had coffee together. It was after the movies. Don't you remember?"

"Yes," she replied, feeling ill as she thought back to that evening. It had seemed so innocent, catching a movie with Gayle and running into Larry outside the theater. She had only invited him to have coffee because she'd known Gayle had a crush on him. Not even when he'd asked her out later, Clea realized, had she suspected his feelings. She cringed as he stroked her hair and danced her around and around the room to music only he could hear.

"You're so beautiful," he told her. "And after tonight, we'll be together always."

He's insane, and he's going to kill me.

Panic rose like bile in her throat. She fought it back. No! She wouldn't let him steal her future from her. Not now. Not when she and Ryan had just found each other. She squeezed her eyes shut. *Think, Clea. Think. There has to be a way out.*

Suddenly he stopped dancing, and she nearly tripped at the abrupt movement. Her eyes popped open, new terror gripping her as she waited to see what he would do next.

"I have another gift for you," he crooned. Reaching into the pocket of his jacket, he pulled out a silky red scarf and draped it around her neck. "I like you in red."

"Thank you. It's pretty," she said, hoping he didn't hear the trembling in her voice. Frantic, her heart pounding with fear, she stared at their reflection in the mirror against the far wall. She eyed the top of the desk behind her, searching for a weapon. Something, anything. She spotted the crystal paperweight with the gold nugget in the center. A gift from her sister Lorelei and her husband Jack. She heard the screech of tires.

"That must be Ryan," she said.

"No," Larry snapped. He caught the ends of the scarf and wrapped it around his fists.

"You'll ruin the scarf, Larry," she told him, fighting back panic. "It'll get all wrinkled if you bunch it up like that. It's so pretty. You wouldn't want to ruin it."

He hesitated a moment, looking confused.

Then she heard it again. Tires screeching. A car door slamming. Fists pounding on the door. Glass smashing. "Clea!"

"Ryan! Ryan, I'm in here!"

"No!" Larry screamed. His eyes turned black, wild with

rage. He wound the scarf around his fists and tightened it around her throat. "You still want him. You would betray me with him. Just like you did before!"

She clawed at his hands, digging her nails into his flesh, drawing blood as she struggled to breathe.

"Clea!" Ryan yelled again. Something hit hard against the door. "Let her go, Granger. Let her go!"

Her vision blurred. She could feel her head growing fuzzy and dark. She fought to clear it.

"Clea!"

Ryan. She had to live for Ryan. Even as she felt consciousness slipping away, she ceased her attack on the hands at her throat to grope for the paperweight behind her on the desk.

"You're mine. Mine," Larry said, pulling the scarf even tighter. "If I can't have you, no one will."

She searched the desk behind her with her fingers, knocking over files. She stuggled to remain conscious. Then she felt the cool, heavy crystal. Closing her fist around it, she thought of Ryan, of the life that stretched out before them, and mustering all the strength she had left, she smashed the paperweight against Larry's head.

He cried out. The pressure around her throat ceased as he released the scarf to grab his bleeding head. Staring down at the blood on his hands and then at her, he staggered back a step—then charged at her again.

Ryan crashed through the door. He let out a cry of rage and grabbed Larry, dragging him off her. And then he began pummeling him with his fists.

Gasping for air, Clea dropped to her knees. The room began to spin. Three hazy images of Ryan swam before her. Two of them pulling one of the Ryans away from Larry. Then she recognized the voices.

"Ry! Ry, let him go," Sean said.

"You can stop hitting him, man. He's unconscious,"

Michael told him. "We'll take care of him. You go see about Clea."

He rushed over to her, gathered her in his arms. His hands touched her face, her hair as though he were afraid she would break. His face was white, his eyes wide with fear. The room was starting to turn gray. So was he.

"Clea. Speak to me. Say something. Oh God, I can't lose you. I love you. You have to be all right."

Her eyes fluttered. She struggled against the ever deepening gray. Reaching out, she touched his face. "I..."

"What? What is it?"

She coughed and tried again, feeling herself begin to slide into that heavy fog. "I love you, too," she managed to whisper. "But you're fired." Then she promptly fainted.

Squinting against the shower of rose petals, Ryan clutched Clea's hand and raced down the steps of the church to the white limo waiting to take them to the wedding reception.

It had been two months since that terrifying night. Gayle had recovered from the overdose of pills Larry had forced down her. And he had seen to it that Larry was put away for a long time. Clea had at last believed him that her infertility didn't matter, and their first appointment with an adoption agency was scheduled after they returned from their honeymoon. Best of all, he had finally made Clea his wife.

"Ready, Mrs. Fitzpatrick?" he asked as they reached the limo.

"Ready."

"Hey, wait a minute. Wait a minute," Michael caught him as he was about to open the car door. "Not so fast, little brother. Sean and I want to make good on our bet."

"Your bet?" Clea repeated, her eyebrows arched in surprise.

"Later, guys. Come on, Clea. They're waiting for us at the reception."

"Don't you want your two hundred bucks? You won it fair and square," Sean said innocently. "Although I still don't understand why she chose you over me."

"I'll collect it later," Ryan said, and opened the door to the limo.

Clea shoved the door closed. "Not so fast, Fitzpatrick. What bet?"

"Just a little wager about the legendary Fitzpatrick charm," Ryan replied.

"Legendary?" she countered.

"Sure. Why don't I give you a demonstration," he offered, and ushered her into the back seat where he proceeded to do just that.

* * * * * *

Sizzling, Sexy, Sun-drenched...

SUMMER SENSATIONS

Three short stories by *New York Times* bestselling authors will heat up your summer!

LINDA HOWARD

LINDA LAEL MILLER

HEATHER GRAHAM POZZESSERE

Experience the passion today!

Available at your favorite retail outlet.

TM

Look us up on-line at: http://www.romance.net

Marie Ferrarella's

RITA Award Winning Author

*miniseries continues with her
brand-new Silhouette single title*

In The Family Way

Dr. Rafe Saldana was Bedford's most popular pediatrician. And though the handsome doctor had a whole lot of love for his tiny patients, his heart wasn't open for business with women. At least, not until single mother Dana Morrow walked into his life. But Dana was about to become the newest member of the Baby of the Month Club. Was the dashing doctor ready to play daddy to her baby-to-be?

Available June 1998.

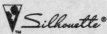

Find this new title by Marie Ferrarella
at your favorite retail outlet.

MEN at WORK

All work and no play? Not these men!

April 1998
KNIGHT SPARKS by Mary Lynn Baxter

Sexy lawman Rance Knight made a career of arresting the bad guys. Somehow, though, he thought policewoman Carly Mitchum was framed. Once they'd uncovered the truth, could Rance let Carly go...or would he make a citizen's arrest?

May 1998
HOODWINKED by Diana Palmer

CEO Jake Edwards donned coveralls and went undercover as a mechanic to find the saboteur in his company. Nothing— or no one—would distract him, not even beautiful secretary Maureen Harris. Jake had to catch the thief—*and* the woman who'd stolen his heart!

June 1998
DEFYING GRAVITY by Rachel Lee

Tim O'Shaughnessy and his business partner, Liz Pennington, had always been close—but never *this* close. As the danger of their assignment escalated, so did their passion. When the job was over, could they ever go back to business as usual?

MEN AT WORK™

Available at your favorite retail outlet!

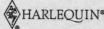 

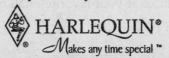

SILHOUETTE®

Desire®

For nearly ten years Silhouette Desire has been giving readers the ultimate in sexy, irresistible heroes. And you'll find those same gorgeous men tempting you to turn every page in the upcoming sensual, emotional **Man of the Month** love stories, written by your favorite authors.

Available at your favorite retail outlet.